Also from Indigo Sea Press
Novels by Leigh Somerville

It All Started with a Dog
Black Magic

indigoseapress.com

All Good Things

The sequel to
IT ALL STARTED WITH A DOG

By

Leigh Somerville

Perseverance Books
Published by Indigo Sea Press
Winston-Salem

Perseverance Books
Indigo Sea Press, LLC
302 Ricks Drive
Winston-Salem, NC 27103

This book is a work of fiction. Names, characters, locations and events are either a product of the author's imagination, fictitious or used fictitiously. Any resemblance to any event, locale or person, living or dead, is purely coincidental.

Copyright 2012 by Leigh Somerville

All rights reserved, including the right of reproduction in whole or part in any format.

First Perseverance Books edition published
January, 2016
Perseverance Books, Moon Sailor and all production design are trademarks of Indigo Sea Press, used under license.

For information regarding bulk purchases of this book, digital purchase and special discounts, please contact the publisher at indigoseapress.com

Cover design by Tracy Beltran

Manufactured in the United States of America
ISBN 978-1-63066-335-3

This book is dedicated to my father,
who taught me the joy of storytelling.

"All good things come to those who wait."
Rachel's grandmother

Chapter One

Rachel peered at three full-length images of herself in the Macy's dressing room mirror. This is ridiculous, she thought.

A 62-year-old never-been-married woman crammed into a small dressing room with acres of white satin and lace. Wedding dresses hung like clouds from brass hooks on the walls around her. Veils draped in mounds on the tiny chair. The dress Rachel had just taken off – the one with the cinched waist and bow perched saucily on her bottom – made her look like Snow White. She handed it out to Susan.

"Susan, this is not going to work."

Susan shoved in another designer gown. "Now, don't you go getting all grumpy on me, Rachel Springer," she said from outside the door. "Of course, this is going to work, and, not only is it going to work, it's going to be fun. We're talking about your wedding here, honey. This is not a court case you're getting ready for. Now, try that lovely creation on, and keep your mind open. We just haven't found the right one yet. Keep at it."

Rachel scooped up a pile of satin and threw it out at Susan. Hangers clattered, bringing the Macy's consultant scurrying out from behind her large mahogany desk. "May I assist you, ladies?" the perfectly powdered and coiffed woman chirped. She stared, wide-eyed and open-mouthed at the sight of Susan buried under the mound of rejects while Rachel crouched behind her, red-faced and sweaty.

Rachel's wedding to John Turner loomed less than a month away. Susan had scheduled the caterer and the musicians. Georgia,

Rachel's law firm secretary, had mailed the invitations. John's tux and a miniature replica for his grandson, Ben, had been ordered. Susan had picked out a beautiful dusty rose silk dress to wear as the matron of honor and found a tiny version of the same dress for Mary, the flower girl. Mary and her mother, Belle Mason, had lived in Rachel's downstairs apartment near Dupont Circle since she rescued them from life on the streets.

The wedding ceremony would be performed in Rachel's living room. All they needed now was a wedding dress.

"Susan, this is silly," Rachel barked from inside the dressing room where she had squeezed herself into a very skinny gown with bare shoulders and a low, scooped neckline. "Look at my turkey neck. I need something high to cover it. And I just can't get beyond the fact that I'm 62 and trying to look like a young virgin."

Susan stepped into closer range and surveyed the scene silently. She tilted her head first one way and then another, squinted, frowned, pursed her lips and scratched her head. She spun Rachel around so she could look at every angle.

"I think we need to cut your hair," she pronounced with a bright smile. "It's your long, gray braid that's the problem."

"John calls it 'silver' and says it's my best asset. He'd never forgive me if I cut it off. Ben would be heartbroken. And, Susan, there's something else we need to talk about. Something I haven't told you."

Susan plopped down on the floor outside the dressing room and laid her head against the wall. She buried her face in her hands.

"You're not backing out are you? Rachel, you can't change your mind now. John's a ..."

"No, I'm not changing my mind about marrying John. Of course not. It's not that."

"Then what is it?" Susan asked, bracing herself for all the possibilities that might ruin the scenario she had planned for the past month.

"I can't wear white. I'm not a virgin."

Susan opened the door and stared at her friend as though she had just heard that Mother Teresa had announced that she was pregnant.

"You've got to be kidding me. Rachel, I've known you for 40 years and you've never even gone out on a date much less …"

"It was a long time ago. A very long time ago. In college."

"Well, that doesn't count, Rachel. My word, you're almost like a virgin now. You're a senior citizen."

"Stop! Stop right there! I don't want to hear another word. Let's get out of here. I'm not going to make a fool of myself in one of these outrageous costumes by pretending to be a blushing bride."

"Rachel, nobody's a virgin these days, and Macy's still sells these dresses by the thousands. Come on, honey, try one more on. We'll find the perfect dress, and John will see you walking toward him like an angel, a vision in white, and you'll …"

"No, absolutely not. I will not do this." Rachel's muffled voice came from inside the fabric. "Help me get out of here. I want to go home."

It wasn't until Susan realized that her friend was in tears that she gave up on her mission to find the perfect dress. At least for that day.

"Well, okay. Maybe we can look at Neiman Marcus tomorrow."

"No, Susan. No more. No more white. No more lace and seed pearls. Most importantly, no more veils. I want to wear something suitable for a 62-year-old non-virgin who is old enough to be the ring bearer's grandmother."

"But it's your first wedding. Don't you want to remember it forever as a fairytale romance? What about the pictures? What about my dress and how it will look beside your dress? What exactly do you have in mind?" Susan had collapsed on the dressing room floor by this time, looking up at her friend like a drowning soul.

"I don't know, Susan, but it's not this."

* * *

Later that afternoon, lying in her garden tub surrounded by bubbles, a glass of white wine within reach, Rachel smiled. Memories of her morning's tragic foray into the world of brides had evolved into the realm of comedy. How wonderful the way time – even a little time – can transform torture into a joke, she thought.

She remembered one of her grandmother's favorite sayings, "This too shall pass."

At least, I didn't spend thousands of dollars to look like a clown, she consoled herself. Of course, she was still left with the problem of what to wear on her wedding day.

"I'll think about it tomorrow," she decided as she stepped out of the water. Drying herself, she looked down at her short stubby legs and remembered another of her grandmother's wise sayings, "As long as they work, don't complain."

Rachel smiled. Yes, the knees had started to sag. Yes, the backs of her thighs dimpled and her crepe paper skin jiggled a little when she walked, but all her parts worked.

She treasured her walk to work every day. The long blocks from Dupont Circle to Georgetown served not only as exercise but as her daily dose of community, thanks to Ralph. The trip from home to office was sprinkled generously with just the right amount of conversation as people stopped to pet the dog and speak to his owner. People she knew – like Deejee, the hotdog vendor – as well as strangers. By the time she unlocked the door to her office, she had enjoyed a dose of the kind of love that got her through her day as a lawyer.

The phone rang just as Rachel finished toweling her hair. She threw on a robe and dashed into the bedroom to answer it. Mrs. Moser was on the other end of the line.

"Afternoon, Rachel," the older woman said. "Hope I didn't catch you at a bad time."

4

"Just stepped out of the bath. Perfect timing."

"Well, I was dying to know about your shopping trip. Did you find a dress?"

"Afraid not. We looked at lots of dresses, but I didn't find a thing that suited me. I think it's hopeless."

Mrs. Moser was silent. Rachel could hear her husband's voice in the background, muttering something she couldn't quite make out.

"Sorry, Rachel. I've been warned not to interfere. Now, you know I'd never do that, don't you, dear? I just wanted to see if you need my help at all. I'd love to go with you shopping any time. A girl needs a mother at a time like this, don't you think?"

Rachel smiled to herself, picturing her little neighbor bustling about, advising her on which veil would go with which dress and why.

"Actually, Mrs. Moser, I think you've hit the nail on the head. You've precisely identified the problem. I'm not a GIRL. I fit more correctly into the mother-of-the-bride role. And that's why this isn't working."

"Oh, dear," Mrs. Moser whispered. "I see what you mean. That IS a problem."

* * *

Later that evening, Rachel, John and Ben arrived at the theater just in time to buy popcorn and drinks and claim Ben's favorite seats on the front row. John had tried to talk his grandson into letting Rachel pick the seats for a change, but she reassured them both that she loved sitting up front with all the kids.

"See, Granddad, I told you so. I told you me and Rachel always like the same things."

John winked across the tousled head at Rachel and settled back for "Up," a new animated film about a little boy who befriends an old man whose wife has just died. The two soar through the last half of the movie in a hot air balloon.

Ben moved in unusual silence out of the dark and into the bright lights of the lobby. They had walked a couple of blocks before anyone spoke.

"Granddad?"

"Yes, Ben."

"I hope Rachel doesn't die."

John looked over at the woman who was soon to be his wife and felt his chest tighten. "I hope so, too, Ben, but I don't think we need to worry. The woman in the movie was very old, and it was time for her to die. Rachel isn't old."

Ben didn't look too convinced about that, but he smiled. "You promise? Rachel's not going to die, right?"

"Well, we certainly hope not, Ben. We hope she'll live a very, very long time."

Rachel leaned down and hugged the child to her in an embrace that reminded her of all the many ways her life had been enriched since the day Susan had introduced her to John. Against her better judgment, she had rented him her basement apartment and, in the process, had learned the joys of sharing. A visit from his grandson had sweetened the deal.

And then came the phone call that changed all their lives forever.

Rachel was visiting her cousins on the family farm when she got the message that Ben's parents had been killed in a car wreck, leaving John Turner custody of his grandson. After the funeral, Rachel asked John and Ben to move upstairs with her so they'd have more room.

The months since then had been full of the joys and frustrations of living with a child.

When Rachel loosened her hold, Ben announced that he had one more question. Rachel and John braced themselves.

"What is it, Ben?" John asked.

"Can we still go on a hot air balloon ride even if Rachel doesn't die?"

John picked his grandson up and plopped him onto his shoulders for the rest of the walk home. "That's about as high as you're going to get right now, mister."

Rachel laughed at the two and tucked her arm through John's. The muscles under his sweater were still firm and bulged just enough to satisfy her taste. What are the chances of a 62-year-old woman who's never been in love finding not only romance but a ready-made family, she asked herself for the millionth time.

The answer was always the same: it all started with a dog.

Rachel found the dog she named "Ralph" one evening as she worked late at her office in Georgetown. Her secretary, Georgia, had gone home, leaving her there alone, preparing another pleading in a long drawn-out divorce case.

When she finally locked the door and stepped out onto the darkening streets, her thoughts wandered, lost in the trials and tribulations of yet another soon-to-be ex-wife who was living proof that "hell hath no fury like that of a woman scorned."

A whining deep in the alleyway next to her office building brought her back to reality. When she walked over to investigate the pitiful sound, all she could see at first were two terrified eyes and the vague outline of an animal. She couldn't tell what kind.

Rachel called out softly, surprised at her willingness to brave an unknown creature hiding in the dark. After a couple of minutes of persistent calling, out from the shadows crept a black dog that looked like he hadn't eaten in months. His fur reminded Rachel of a moth-eaten mink coat she'd found years ago in her grandmother's attic. The dog peered up at her with eyes that begged for help.

Against Rachel's better judgment – and to the chagrin of a heavily tipped driver – the stray rode away in the back seat of the

Yellow Cab, beginning a chain of events that all worked toward the slow transformation of Rachel Springer.

Never much of a dog person, Rachel was surprised at the impact this one had on her life and everyone they met. Their daily walks inspired a sense of community she had never known before. And clients seemed to relax and open up as soon as they saw Ralph sitting in the front window. After several months of being the recipient of his unconditional love, Rachel found herself willing to do all kinds of risky things. Like taking in a downstairs tenant and then falling in love – first with the little boy and then with his grandfather.

Yes, it all started with a dog, she said as she looked at John and Ben, charging up the steps to open their front door for her. As if on cue, Ralph dashed out with kisses for all.

Chapter Two

T he phone rang as Rachel walked into her office early the next morning. Georgia had taken the day off to meet her son and his family at the airport, leaving Rachel to answer her own calls.

Susan was on the other end. In her typical fashion, she launched right into the purpose of her call with no preamble.

"Got time for lunch today? I've got something I need to talk to you about."

Rachel looked at her calendar, surprised to see that she had a couple of free hours around noon. "Sure. Where do you want to meet?"

"Here. We need to be private."

"Okay, but can you give me at least a clue as to what this is all about?"

Susan had already hung up by the time Rachel finished the sentence. The two had been friends since they met as students at the University of Virginia 40 years ago. Rachel knew this lunch meeting could run the gamut from what to serve at a dinner party to questions about how to plan World War III.

Susan was a no-holds-barred kind of woman, and Rachel never knew what to expect from her. Recently, she had called with a question about where to take hang-gliding lessons. What puzzled Rachel was the need for privacy. Susan was such an open book most of the time. Childlike in the way she trusted everybody.

But with a new client coming in five minutes, Rachel didn't have time to ponder the purpose of the meeting with Susan. She needed to find the new client forms and couldn't remember where Georgia kept them.

As she stood at her secretary's desk, she smiled at the photographs scattered across the top and taped to the wall behind it. Will and Georgia on their 25th wedding anniversary cruise. Her son, his wife and their twin boys sitting under a Christmas tree. The family playing at the beach. The family in front of their new house.

Rachel remembered the days when the pictures had occasionally created a sense of longing in her. Not often, but at times, she felt a vague awareness of what was missing in her life. Despite all her degrees, her financial stability, her friends and interests, she sometimes felt a gaping hole. Looking at the evidence of Georgia's full family life created a contrast that dug the hole even deeper.

Ralph had changed all that. Shortly after the dog arrived, Georgia had taken a picture of Rachel and him sitting on the steps of her three-story brownstone. As a surprise, she had it framed and sat it in a place of honor beside the telephone on Rachel's desk. As pictures of Ben and John joined it, the black hole had disappeared along with them.

Lost in her gratefulness, Rachel jumped in surprise when the office door opened and a tall blonde poked her head inside.

"Is this Springer and Associates?"

"Yes, come on in. I'm Rachel Springer."

The young woman entered, pulling a briefcase on wheels behind her. Dressed in a smart black business suit, she was model perfect. Rachel admired the ease with which she maneuvered on her stiletto heels.

"Have a seat. I'm looking for the intake form for you to fill out. My secretary has taken the day off. You'll have to bear with me a minute while I find it."

"No problem," the young woman said, taking a seat in the

rocking chair and picking up one of Georgia's old *Good Housekeeping* magazines.

Rachel found the form in a folder carefully labeled "Intake," right where it should be, filed alphabetically after "Heath Insurance." She invited her potential client into her inner office and closed the door. The woman seemed to hesitate in making a choice about a seat that would provide room for her briefcase.

"Here, let me move this table, and you can sit here," Rachel said.

"Thanks. And I'm sorry. I don't think I've even introduced myself. I'm Carrie Johnson." Carrie Johnson reached out her hand, and Rachel shook it.

"Why don't you take a minute to fill out that form, and I'll get us some coffee. I just brewed it. What do you take in yours?"

"Black, please."

"That's always a relief since I'm a black coffee drinker, myself," Rachel said. On the way to the kitchen, she wondered how Georgia managed to get just the right amount of cream and sugar in everybody's coffee. Georgia filled many roles in Rachel's life. Ace secretary was only one. She also filled the void left in Rachel's life after her mother died when she was 10 years old. On the days when Georgia's chair sat empty, Rachel felt like a force had sucked all the life out of the office.

Rachel noticed a few chocolate chip cookies left on a plate covered with Saran wrap and debated whether it was too early in the morning to serve them. Deciding that Georgia would definitely do so, she carried the plate on a tray with the two cups of coffee.

Carrie Johnson leaned forward and reached for the tray, relieved to have something to focus on other than the issue that had brought her to Springer & Associates. Now I know why Georgia always has chocolate chip cookies around, Rachel thought.

"So what can I do to help you?" she asked, glancing down at the neat handwriting spilling over the lines on the form and into the margins.

Carrie uncrossed her long, shapely legs, shimmering in fine silk hose colored sheer black. She leaned over and opened the briefcase to reveal several very large notebooks. She removed one and placed it carefully on Rachel's desk. She pushed it across the wide expanse to Rachel and leaned back in her seat with a sigh. Her shoulders dropped as though she'd just handed over the weight of the world.

Rachel waited patiently while the woman across from her took a bite of cookie and followed it with several sips of coffee. She dabbed at the corners of her mouth.

"What you see there is documentation of my grandfather's research. Careful notes about the experiments he conducted over the period of about four years. The last notebook details an invention I believe has been stolen from him."

Rachel took a gulp of her own coffee, stalling for time. She hated research. Science of any kind was her worst nightmare. Georgia, while entirely capable of doing just about anything, didn't have time for research. And there was no one else in the office onto whom she could shift the work of reading through all the documents lying in front of her in their dusty black binders.

Rachel leaned forward and opened the cover in front of her. In a thin spidery script written in fading black ink were the bold words "Jonathan Green Johnson. Date: December 24, 1947. TOP SECRET."

That stopped her. She looked up at Carrie.

"I don't usually practice intellectual property law," she said. "It's not my specialty. There are many other attorneys much more qualified to help you than I am. I'd be happy to give you the names of a few."

Carrie looked crestfallen. She stood up and approached the desk. "Mrs. Springer, I came to you because I was told you could help me. I was told you are the best."

"Who referred you?"

"Horace Gilbert."

Rachel took another sip of coffee. She drained the cup and set it down beside her carefully. She certainly didn't want to get on the wrong side of Horace by turning this young woman away. Half her time was spent getting him out of one jam after another. At the moment, his problem was beyond her scope of expertise, however.

Horace lay in a hospital across town recovering from quadruple bypass surgery after the heart attack his doctors had warned him about for years. Rachel didn't want to upset him by rejecting this case. She wondered how Carrie knew him and decided to buy herself some more time by asking.

"So, how do you know Horace?"

"His son, Horace Junior, and I are engaged to be married."

It's even worse than I thought, Rachel thought. "Congratulations," she said. "When's the wedding?"

"A month from now."

"How lovely. I'm getting married in a month, too. Got your dress yet?"

The young woman's mouth dropped open in horror. "Oh, yes. I've had it for about six months. Had it especially designed for me by a friend. She made it using parts of my grandmother's wedding dress. Jonathan's wife."

Rachel thought about her own wedding dress predicament and sifted through her mental wardrobe to see if she could find the makings of a wedding ensemble there. Nothing came to mind.

"How about you? What are you wearing?" Carrie asked politely.

"Haven't found anything yet. Still looking."

Carrie avoided Rachel's eyes, as though she had just been told that the groom had a fatal disease. She nodded sympathetically. "Good luck," she said, but her expression looked far from hopeful.

"Well, let's get back to why you're here. What's your grandfather's invention? Must be significant for you to want to spend the money to protect it. This won't be cheap, you must know," Rachel said, indicating the volumes in front of her.

"I don't really know much other than it involves electrical engineering and several friends have warned me that someone else has claimed the patent," Carrie said and waited for Rachel's response.

"Well, as I told you, science is not in my realm of knowledge or expertise. I'd have to hire someone to read all this, and that's going to cost a lot of money. Don't you want to hire someone who knows about this sort of thing?"

"Horace said to come to you. He said I could trust you. That's the most important thing to me. Trust."

Rachel agreed that trust was important. Still, the thought of working on a case that involved electrical engineering was more than she could swallow.

"I know this isn't the kind of case you normally handle, Mrs. Springer ..."

"It's Ms.," Rachel interrupted, "but please call me Rachel."

"Rachel, thanks. I need to prove that Grandfather invented this first." Carrie stood up and took out her checkbook. "I'll pay you in advance right now. How much do you want?"

Rachel looked at her watch and was surprised at how much time had passed. If Georgia had been in her position of command, she would have made some excuse to interrupt by now to move things along. Rachel's second appointment was due to arrive in five minutes.

"I'll tell you what," Rachel said, "leave these notebooks with me overnight. I'll take a look at them and call you with my decision tomorrow. Fair enough?"

"Thank you, Rachel. I knew I could count on you."

"Now, wait a minute. I didn't say I'd do it. Just that I'd consider it."

"Thanks. I was so afraid you'd turn me down before you even looked through the notebooks."

I probably should, Rachel thought, but she didn't.

* * *

Rather than walking, Rachel hailed a cab and rode to Susan's house. Even the metro would eat up more time than she had allowed herself for lunch. She wanted to get back to the office and take a look at Carrie's stash of notebooks before her afternoon appointments began.

Like the Energizer bunny, Susan swept the sidewalk in front of her house as the cab pulled alongside the curb beside her. Rachel chuckled to herself at her friend's outfit for the day. A 1950s Betty Crocker-style bib apron, shiny black patent leather tap shoes and a lavender fleece jogging suit.

"You're the picture of domestic bliss," Rachel announced as she stepped out of the cab. She tipped the cabbie and waved to Belle and Mary across the street. The young woman and her toddler had returned home from grocery shopping and were headed down the steps to Rachel's basement apartment with their bags.

"You were a brave woman to take those two in," Susan said. "Not sure if I would have done it. Homeless. Living on the street. And then that nightmarish incident when her no-good boyfriend showed up at your house drunk in the middle of the night. Whatever happened to him?"

"All quiet on that front. I think the restraining order scared him. The last thing he wants is legal trouble. Belle says he's got a pretty checkered past."

"So does Belle, right?"

"Yes, but look at her now. Gone back to school. Working on a degree. And I don't know what we'd do without her. She and Mary have become the family Ben lost."

Susan was quiet. She swept some leaves off the sidewalk into a pile she had started making near the porch. Since speechless was rarely part of Susan's repertoire, Rachel suspected trouble. She allowed her friend to sweep on in silence for a few minutes and enjoyed the scratch of the broom as it moved back and forth.

I know why Zen masters make sweeping a meditation practice, Rachel thought. With each swipe of the broom, she could feel the tension ease from her shoulders.

Susan interrupted her meditation with a playful pat on Rachel's bottom with the broom. "Come on in. Let's eat. We've got some talking to do."

Susan led the way through her long hallway to the breakfast room at the back of her house. She had laid out two brightly colored and handcrafted ceramic plates, bought during a recent trip to Mexico. The afternoon sun fell directly on them, making them seem to leap off the table. Bright red-orange poppies stood in a tall turquoise vase in the center of the table.

"I've fixed a Caesar salad with last night's leftover chicken on it. Have a seat. I'll go get the food."

Rachel sat facing Susan's backyard, so different from her own across the street. Enclosed by a high brick wall and filled with flower beds, container gardens and a cherub fountain as its focal point, Rachel's courtyard provided a haven of urban privacy. In comparison, Susan's had been copied from a picture of suburbia. Lush green grass made a soft carpeted expanse that started at the back stoop and extended all the way to her neighbor's yard on the street behind. A swing set had been planted in the middle of the yard, and a sandbox in an area to the left. Susan loved her role as grandmother.

"So, when did you lose your virginity?" she asked, plopping down a glass of sweet tea.

"Excuse me?"

16

"You said you didn't want to wear a white dress. COULDN'T wear a white dress. Because you're not a virgin. So, as your best friend, what I want to know is when did this happen? I thought you and John were waiting."

Rachel took another sip of tea and wiped her mouth on the edge of the bright orange linen napkin. She laid it in a neat square beside her empty plate. "Well, Susan, I'm not sure this is any of your business."

"What do you mean 'none of my business?' I'm your matron of honor. I'm almost your mother, for goodness sake."

Susan looked hurt, like her favorite toy had just been smashed to the floor at her feet. When her bottom lip started to tremble, Rachel reached over and patted her on the hand. "Susan, my gosh, it's no big deal. It was years ago. My college sweetheart. At the beach."

"Under the boardwalk?"

"Okay, under the boardwalk. On a beach blanket, if you want."

"Were you drunk?"

"Absolutely not. We were just young."

"And in love?"

"We thought we were. I know now we were just two children with a new toy."

Susan nodded her head like she remembered the new toy. "It'll be very different with John," she said, gazing out at the backyard where Ralph lay in the shade under the weeping willow. "Very different."

"I won't ask any questions," Rachel said. "Unless you need to talk about something. Do you?"

Susan stood to clear the table. Rachel knew not to press the issue. Susan wasn't one to be pressed. When she was ready to talk, she'd talk. She walked back to the table, carrying a plate of brownies dusted with confectioner's sugar.

"Just like my grandmother used to make," Rachel said, choosing the smallest square on the plate.

"Yes, and I think your grandmother would want you to wear white, Rachel. I'm sure of it."

"How do you know? You never even met my grandmother."

"Well, I feel like I know her. You talk about her all the time. 'No rest for the weary' and 'this too shall pass.' A woman like that would want her only granddaughter to wear a white, traditional wedding gown. I'm sure of it. Trust me on this."

"I fail to follow your reasoning, Susan, but I'll keep thinking about it. In the meantime, I need to take Ralph back across the street and get to the office. I'm late already."

Susan shoved a second brownie at her friend and opened the back door.

"Wait, I've got something else for you," she said disappearing into the den. As Rachel rounded the corner of the house with Ralph trailing behind her, Susan dashed out the front door. She shoved the latest issue of *Bride* magazine at her, saying "Here, read this and call me in the morning."

18

Chapter Three

W hen Rachel opened the front door to let Ralph back inside, she heard the phone ring. She was tempted to let it go unanswered. Nobody knew she was home. Must be a telemarketer. But her curiosity got the better of her, and she grabbed the receiver off the hook on the last ring.

"Hello?"

"You sound breathless. You all right?" John asked.

Rachel laughed. "I tried not to answer the phone and then had to run in here to get it when I changed my mind." Rachel eased down on the stool beside the wall phone. "What's going on with you?"

"Just wanted to remind you that Ben has a sleepover with Charlie tonight, and I'm looking forward to spending a romantic evening alone with you."

Rachel pushed a loose strand of hair behind her ear and stood up to look at herself in the hall mirror. She didn't think she looked like a woman who might inspire romantic thoughts, but perhaps if she got rid of the black jacket and serious shoes, she might.

"Rachel, are you there?"

"I'm sorry. Guess I'm a little distracted. New client came in today with a very technical case, and I've just had lunch with Susan."

"Well, maybe you'd like to stay at home tonight, order a pizza and rent a movie. Sound good?"

"Sounds great. Sure you don't mind?"

"As long as we can keep in the romance."

"We can keep in the romance. I'll be home by six." Rachel hung up the phone and dashed down the street to the corner where she usually had no trouble hailing a cab at that time of the day. After about 10 minutes of not seeing even one taxi, she started to walk to the metro station. The day was sunny and cooler than normal for the time of year. Her study of a squirrel perched in a tree above her was interrupted by the blast of a car horn.

"Need a ride, lady?" Rachel turned to frown at the rudeness and was surprised to see Stan Berninger stopped in the middle of his lane, holding up traffic. Rachel opened the private investigator's passenger door, as much to get traffic moving as to hitch a ride.

"Hey, Stan. What are you doing over on this side of town?"

"Met a friend at Zorba's for lunch," he said, adding a belch for emphasis. Stan was not the kind to apologize. He was the kind to lay both hands on the horn as a city bus pulled in front of him.

"Sonovabitch," he yelled out the window. "Sorry, Rachel. These bus drivers think just because they're bigger than everyone else they can do whatever the hell they want to do."

Rachel smiled to herself but didn't point out that her friend had caused a minor traffic jam by stopping in the middle of the road to speak to her.

"So, what are you doing home in the middle of the day?" he asked.

"Lunch with Susan. She's trying to help me decide on what to wear to the wedding."

Stan had been thrilled when Rachel asked his granddaughter Lily to be the second flower girl. Since then, he had taken a personal interest in all the wedding plans.

"Well, what's the problem? You go down to Metro Center and you try on dresses and you pick one out and you buy it. Simple."

"Stan, I'm 62 years old. It's not simple. I look like I've lost my mind in those dresses. They're just not me. I can't do it."

Stan stared at Rachel for a minute or two and then said, "You know what, Rachel? I think you might be right."

* * *

When she walked into her office, Rachel was still chuckling to herself at the look of horror on Stan's face as he contemplated the vision of her in a wedding dress. She wasn't sure whether she was relieved that he agreed with her or insulted. Neither position helped. She still didn't know what to wear.

The pile of notebooks on her desk brought her back to the moment and to the more immediate challenge of whether to take the intellectual property case. She set her pocketbook on the chair in front of her desk and took her seat behind it to check the answering machine messages.

Whenever Georgia took time away from the office, Rachel wondered how her secretary managed to do all she did. The answering machine had recorded five messages during the hour and a half she had been gone.

Springer & Associates was a busy practice. Occasionally, Rachel considered making the name of the firm legitimate by hiring another lawyer. During the years she had practiced in her own firm, she had never let the idea go beyond a minor temptation. She knew herself very well, and one of the things she knew without a doubt was that she played best by herself.

Which was also why she'd never been married.

And now here she was about to become a wife AND a stepmother. Was she losing her mind?

She told herself she enjoyed coming home to the smell of supper cooking. And there was nothing like having a little boy in the house to make you feel young again. She had enjoyed all the trips to the zoo and the museums she had never visited. She loved playing

Chinese checkers and reading Winnie the Pooh. Rachel felt like she'd been given her childhood back. And when Ben rested his little head in her lap as she read to him, she knew deeply that all was well with the world.

Living alone looked pretty lonely at those times.

And working alone looked insane as she began to wade through the phone messages. She was relieved when two turned out to be hang-ups, one from a telemarketer offering her a free weekend at a Williamsburg timeshare resort and one from Georgia reminding her to water the peace lily before she left the office. The last message was the only one that required any action.

Horace's secretary called to demand that she be at his hospital bedside the next morning at nine o'clock.

Rachel considered pretending that she hadn't gotten the message but, knowing Horace, he'd probably call her at home that night. He didn't give up easily, which was, no doubt, why he was lying in the hospital, recovering from open-heart surgery.

Rachel dialed his office number, spoke briefly to his secretary and duly noted the appointment on her personal calendar and the one out front on Georgia's desk.

"Any idea what Horace needs to talk to me about that can't wait until he gets back to the office?" she had asked Horace's latest pretty young secretary.

"No, ma'am. He just said to tell you it would be the most important thing on your calendar tomorrow."

Right, Rachel thought and said good-bye. It always is. At least in Horace's mind.

Rachel knew Horace well enough to expect to be grilled about Carrie Johnson, so she sat down at her desk and opened up the first notebook. Within minutes, she was lost in the spidery handwriting that swept across page after yellowing page of notes and drawings. The man was a storyteller first and a scientist second.

His writing wasn't what Rachel remembered of science labs. No dry, cryptic formulas and hypotheses lacking adjectives and adverbs. Carrie's grandfather spun tales of high drama that kept Rachel engrossed in hypothetical uses for his contraption for hours. She was surprised when the phone rang, jolting her from her reading. She had been at it for two hours and had skimmed through three of the four notebooks already.

"Hello?" Rachel said into the phone, slapping a yellow sticky note on a page to mark her place. "Springer and Associates."

"I'm at the video store," John said. "What movie do you want me to rent?"

"You choose," she said.

John wasn't accustomed to Rachel's indecision. "Sure you don't want a vote?" he asked.

"No, I trust you," she said, warmed to her core at how good those words felt.

* * *

As Rachel neared her house, she smelled chipotle sauce. John knew her favorite foods, or at least one of them – turkey meatloaf smothered in the spicy sauce – and the aroma drifted down the hall toward her as she walked in the front door.

"Honeeeeeee, I'm hooooooome," she sang as she drew near the kitchen. The smells grew stronger with each step, drawing her toward the stove where John stood, stirring a pot of another favorite – collard greens.

He laid the spoon down on the counter and took her into his arms.

"How did I get so lucky?" Rachel asked, her cheek nestled against his strong chest. "And how did you learn to cook? That's probably an easier question to answer."

"It's a long story for another time, my love. For now, how was your day?"

"I had a good day, especially this part of it."

"Well have a seat, milady, and allow me to serve you."

Rachel tossed her jacket on the empty chair near the refrigerator and settled herself on one side of the table. John sat across from her. The third chair remained empty except for the phone book Ben used as a booster seat.

"Was Ben excited about the sleepover?" Rachel asked.

"Beside himself. His only problem was leaving Ralph. I had a time explaining that some folks don't think of Ralph the way we do. As a member of the family. He was sure they'd want him to join the party."

Rachel laughed. "Maybe you should have told them Ralph's a therapy dog. He certainly fills that role."

"In many ways," John said as he heaped Rachel's plate with rice and collard greens. The platter of turkey meatloaf sat in the middle of the table as if it were an offering to the gods. John had garnished it with pansies from the courtyard. Rachel smiled and reached over to pat his hand.

"Thank you," she said, and the two smiled at each other and sat in silence, thinking their own thoughts of gratitude. No words. Just touch. Rachel drank in the fading freckles, the clear green eyes, the graying hair and thought, I've waited a lifetime for this. Thank God, I waited.

"Here, eat up! Your food's getting cold, woman," John said, interrupting her thoughts. "I've slaved all day over a hot stove to prepare this feast for you, and you're getting ready to ruin it sitting there all moony-eyed."

Rachel laughed and took a bite of meatloaf. "Okay, now I'm ready for the story of how you learned to cook."

John took several bites of food, eyes downcast.

"You've heard the saying, 'Necessity is the mother of invention,' right?"

Rachel nodded, chewing in silence.

"Well, that's how I learned to cook. My wife stopped, and I started."

Rachel had heard the story of John's wife's alcoholism. About coming home from work every day to find his wife passed out on the couch, the television blaring, the house dark, his son locked in his bedroom, escaping the scene below.

"I'm surprised you enjoy it so much. I'd think the very idea of having to cook would trigger terrible memories."

"Guess I'm of the opinion that I have a choice. I decided to think of cooking as fun. I took cooking classes and learned to prepare food my son and I loved to eat. Turkey meatloaf with chipotle sauce was one of our favorites, and I decided to use cooking as a way to trick myself into looking forward to coming home after work. Instead of dreading finding my wife drunk, I focused on the kitchen, playing with food. Now when I cook, it's even more fun because I'm cooking for you."

"John Turner, you're an amazing man, and I love you." Rachel thought of her father and how he had taught her to cook after her mother's death. For a 10-year-old girl, it had only represented loss. The deep, dark pit of a child who realizes she'll never feel her mother's arms again. See her smile. Smell her mother's earth smell. As an adult, she had tried to enjoy cooking, but sometimes, even with the opening of a can, Rachel felt that hole open up. Strange how people handle loss differently, she thought.

"But enough of that," John said. "Tell me about your new client."

"My POTENTIAL new client. Despite what Horace thinks, I may not be the best lawyer to help this woman."

Rachel launched into the story between bites of meatloaf and on

25

into homemade apple pie with vanilla ice cream. She told John about the stack of notebooks she had spent the afternoon reading. About the proposed uses for the invention and the many failed but meticulously documented experiments.

"So, in the end, did he succeed?" John asked, eyes wide like a child who's just watched a magic trick.

"I haven't gotten to the end yet. I'm still reading. And the problem is that not much of it makes sense to me. I never did very well in science classes."

John looked at her. He didn't say a word. He sat still and stared at the woman across the table, waiting.

"What? Why are you looking at me like that?" Rachel asked.

John smiled but didn't say a word.

"Okay, I give up," Rachel said. "What is it? What am I missing?"

"Rachel, what do I do for a living?"

"You're an engineer," Rachel said and then laughed. "Duhhhhh. You're a scientist. Guess I never think of you in that way. And I have a hard time seeing the obvious sometimes."

"And asking for help?"

"Well, yes. But are you interested? And do you have time to go through all those notebooks? There are stacks of them. I spent three hours this afternoon, and I'm nowhere near finished."

Rachel didn't say it, but she also questioned the wisdom of working with John. Their love felt so solid. She had heard the horror stories of lovers who tried to combine their personal and professional lives and failed miserably. She simply wasn't willing to risk what she had with John on an intellectual property case.

"Yes, I have time. Sounds like fun. Let me have a crack at it."

"I guess I'll need to get permission from my client first."

"What's the matter? Don't you trust me?" John looked like a little boy who's just been told he couldn't play with a friend's Tinker Toys.

26

"Of course, I trust you. It's standard procedure. Nothing personal." Rachel reached over and kissed John on the cheek. He didn't look like he believed her. See, problems already, she thought. "Let's clear up this mess and get to the movie," she said, carrying her bowl to the dishwasher. "What did you get?"

"Harry Potter," John snapped.

This may have been a mistake, Rachel thought.

"Maybe we should just skip the movie and move on to the romance," she said.

"Maybe we should," John said and switched off the overhead light.

Chapter Four

When Rachel walked into Horace's hospital room the next morning, she could barely see her client behind all the flowers. Horace was a manly man. More than six feet tall and weighing in at more than 300 pounds, his shoulders were broad, his face red and his nose bulbous. He had played fullback on the Virginia Tech football team and still bulldozed his way through life like he was on the field, moving toward the goal post. Plowing through the defensive line.

Rachel flinched at the sight of him in pajamas. She averted her eyes, focusing instead on a huge arrangement of red roses.

"Smells like a damn funeral parlor in here," Horace bellowed. "Sit over here," he boomed, stabbing a finger in the direction of the latest in a long line of young secretaries sitting beside his bed. "Get up, Jessica. Let Rachel have that seat. Why don't you take a break? Go get us some coffee. Rachel, you want coffee?"

"Sir, you're not supposed to drink coffee," the young woman squeaked.

"That's bullshit. Of course, I'm going to drink coffee. Tell them to make it extra strong. Not any of that watered down stuff they bring in here. Tastes like horse piss."

Jessica skittered out of the room, shooting Rachel a look that said, "Save me" on her way out the door.

"Horace, it doesn't sound like you're doing what the doctor ordered," Rachel said.

"Why start now?" he laughed.

"How about because you've had a heart attack?"

"Well, they've fixed me now. I'm sure not going to waste all this time in the hospital and then get out and not be able to do what I want to do. What's the point of living?"

Rachel knew not to argue.

"So, what did you want to see me about?"

"First, what did you think of Carrie? First class, isn't she? First class. I know you are going to do a fine job for her."

When Rachel started to tell Horace that she hadn't decided whether she'd handle the case or not, he interrupted her. Blew off her excuses. Offered to pay her double her regular fee to take on the new client.

"But, Horace ..."

"I know you'll do the right thing, Rachel. You've never let me down. Let's get down to business here. My business," he said as he pulled a red folder out from beneath the mattress. "Here's some notes I want you to look over."

"What's this about, Horace? Give me some idea."

"My will."

Rachel's mouth dropped open. For years, she had tried to talk Horace into writing a will but had never been able to break down his belief that he'd live forever. Or that he'd take it all with him.

Rachel resisted the urge to smile as she leafed through the pages of notes in the red folder. No surprises, really. An even distribution among his two children. A list of charities that wasn't as long as it could have been, considering the man's immense fortune amassed over decades of wise real estate development in a city that had enough money to support it even in bad times. The government always seemed to be able to find funds for a new building when it was needed.

It was only when Rachel came to the last page that she stopped and read carefully the paragraph written in Horace's large bold script. "And to Carrie Johnson I leave The Gilbert Companies and my Virginia Tech class ring."

"What's wrong" Horace barked. "Something wrong with the wording? Fix it. You know what to do with all that mess. Clean it up, put it in one of those stupid blue folders, and I'll sign it tomorrow."

Rachel closed the folder and looked at the man who had held the distinction of being her oldest and most lucrative client ever since she started the firm. Suddenly, he looked old. She reached over and patted the hand lying in a fist on the sheet.

"Nothing's wrong, Horace. I just hadn't ever heard you mention this young woman and all of the sudden you're leaving her your company and a ring that I know means a great deal to you."

"Yes."

"What's it all about? She's marrying your son. Why this special gift to her, rather than to the two of them?"

"Not that it's any of your business, Rachel ..."

"Of course not."

"But her father and I were college roommates and fraternity brothers. He was my best friend. In many ways, he was my brother."

"I think it's wonderful that you feel so close to his daughter that you'd remember her like this. I'm sure she'll be very grateful."

"It's the least I could do after ..." Horace stopped in mid-sentence. "Can you have it ready to sign tomorrow?"

Rachel said she'd have to ask Georgia about her workload. "She's been out of the office, and I'm not sure what she's got backed up on her desk. You know preparing a will is more than typing your notes, Horace." Rachel had gotten beyond the point of feeling insulted by Horace's opinion that any fool could do what most lawyers did and that he was being seriously overcharged for her legal work. Lots of legal work, a steady stream fed by his many sometimes-shady dealings. In the early days, she had confronted the man after he questioned a bill, asserting in no uncertain terms that he could find another lawyer if he didn't think she was worth her hourly rate. Finally, they'd gotten to the point where the conversations had stopped, and he paid his bills without questioning every nickel and dime she charged him.

"Okay, Rachel," Horace grumbled, flicking on the television that hung like a giant bat from the ceiling opposite his bed. The visit was obviously over. "Just don't take too long."

Evidently, Horace's heart attack had more of a sobering effect than her client was willing to admit, Rachel thought. Maybe he was finally ready to acknowledge his mortality.

"Right," Rachel said. "Anything I can get you before I leave?

"Yeah, go find Jessica. That girl's been gone long enough to find the lost city of Atlantis. All I asked for was a damn cup of coffee."

As if on cue, the little blond popped through the door, carrying two cups of steaming coffee. When she realized that Rachel was preparing to leave, she hunched her shoulders as if to protect herself from an attack. As if she thought Horace might fire her on the spot. Rachel felt sorry for the girl. Others had lost the same job for equally minor infractions.

"I'm so sorry, Miss Springer. They had to brew a fresh pot. I had to wait. I didn't know what to do. I guess I could have driven over to Starbucks, but I was afraid …"

"Shut up, Jessica. Rachel doesn't want to hear all that whining."

"It's okay, Jessica. I'm fine. Thanks for trying. I've probably had enough stimulation for one morning anyway," Rachel said and aimed a ferocious frown in Horace's direction. "Take it easy, Horace. I'll call your office when this is ready."

Horace grunted and took a gulp of steaming coffee.

* * *

Rachel beamed when she saw Georgia back at her desk, sitting behind a pile of mail from the day before. She had opened and sorted the contents into two piles. Rachel had never been able to convince her secretary to throw junk mail away. She insisted that Rachel look through it all. Only then was she comfortable tossing it.

"You just never know. There might be something there you need. Some little jewel hiding in the rough. Some secret that might shed light on a case you're working on. Some …"

"Okay, okay, Georgia. I give up. I'll look at it all." Rachel had known from the early days of Georgia's employment that she had met her match on some fronts. When Georgia felt strongly about an issue, there was no talking her out of her position.

Rachel sorted through the junk pile of mail as quickly as she could get away with it and still satisfy her secretary.

"How are Will Junior and the family? Everybody happy to be at Grammy's house?"

"The twins have grown so much. I hardly recognized them. They're walking and talking up a storm. The family is going to stop by here some time this afternoon on their way to the river. The boys want to see boats. How's Horace?"

"You're not going to believe this," Rachel said dropping the red file folder on Georgia's desk. "He wants a will written."

Georgia looked up from the mail as though Rachel had just told her Elvis had a three o'clock appointment.

"And he wants the will prepared today. I told him you'd get to it when you could."

Georgia opened the folder and flipped through the pages of notes. When she came to the last page, she stopped and read carefully. "Who's Carrie Johnson?"

Rachel told her the story, complete with the latest chapter involving the upcoming wedding to Horace's son, the stolen invention and the connection between Horace and Carrie's father.

"So, what do you think?" she asked.

Georgia rose from her chair, walked around the desk and stood in front of her boss. She took both of Rachel's shoulders in her firm grip and looked her in the eye.

"Rachel Springer, I think there's more here than meets the eye."

She didn't say anything more.

"And?"

"I think Horace isn't telling you something. Something important. Something about his relationship with Carrie's father."

"But, what does that have to do with the will?"

"Nothing. I'll prepare the will. Should be able to get it done in a couple of weeks. In the meantime, if I were you, I'd look very carefully for anything that smacks of Horace in those notebooks," Georgia said, walking over to water the wilting peace lily.

* * *

Several hours later as Rachel walked down O Street toward home, she saw Susan standing on her front porch watering the two giant Boston ferns hanging on each side of her door. Water poured from the hole in the bottom of one. Ralph sat beneath it, lapping up the puddle at his feet.

"Don't you ever give your dog any water? He's the drinkingest dog I've ever seen. Is there something wrong with him? Ralph is there something wrong with you?" Susan cooed, crouching down beside him and scratching his ears.

Rachel set her briefcase down on the sidewalk, thinking that the perfect ending to a day at work was coming home to find her best friend outside welcoming her home.

When the "For Sale" sign went up in the yard across the street from her, Susan immediately called Rachel and convinced her to look at the house. Rachel had been living in a condo in Crystal City for years and had no desire to move. But the thought of living across the street from Susan tempted her to make an appointment to see the property. The third floor attic space had tipped the scales. She visualized using it as a meditation room, something she lacked in her small condo across the Potomac. And the cherub fountain in the back courtyard sealed the deal.

The two women, already fast friends, became even closer after Rachel's move. Not a day went by that they didn't visit, at least on the phone. Rachel could read Susan's moods like a book. Today's was mid-summer sunny, no rain in sight.

"So, how was your day?" she chirped. "Any exciting stories to tell poor little homebound me?"

"Right. You're about as poor and little and homebound as Sally Ride. You're probably the one with stories to tell. All I did worth repeating was visit Horace in the hospital."

"How is he?"

"Mean as ever. I can understand why he goes through secretaries so fast. I doubt this latest one will last long."

Susan sat down on the top step with a plop, her eyes dancing, a giggle escaping her as though she were a child who's just discovered how to blow a bubble.

"I know just what that old fart needs, Rachel."

"What does Horace need, Susan? I'm sure you know."

"He needs a poem." Susan looked suddenly serious. Like she was on a mission. "I'll just go right on over there after supper with my notebook and pencils and sit down beside that man's bed and I'll compose one for him right on the spot. I'll get inspired there in his room. I'll —"

Rachel stood up and picked up her briefcase. "You do that, Susan. But let me warn you, the man's been drinking black coffee against doctor's orders, and he's got dying on his mind."

"There you go. That's a great title for my poem. 'Dying on My Mind.'"

"Right. That's sure to cheer him up," Rachel called back over her shoulder as she crossed the street with Ralph.

The door flew open and Ben jumped down the steps into her arms. Ralph tried to lick both of them at once.

"Careful there, boys, you're going to knock Rachel off her feet," John said, joining the happy pile of dog and boy. Rachel laughed.

"Wow, what a welcome. You guys sure know how to make a girl feel loved."

"We do love you, don't we Ralph? Lots and lots." Ralph wagged his tail in agreement and then led the way inside the house.

"Looks like somebody's hungry," John said. "How about you, Rachel? In the mood for vegetable soup?"

"Granddad and I made it ourselves," Ben squealed. "And we did not put any onions in it."

Rachel remembered a scene shortly after Ben's parents died when she had made the mistake of putting onions in the meatloaf. The child had thrown a temper tantrum at the table. "My mommy never makes me eat onions," he had screamed and run off to his room.

Rachel and John had worked with Ben consistently since then, encouraging him to talk about his feelings, especially about how he missed his parents. At first, he had insisted they reserve two seats for them at the table, pretending their angels were there. Recently, he had told Rachel she didn't need to set the two places anymore. The angels had gone on to heaven now, he said.

"But, they're still watching me," he insisted.

"They'll always be watching you, honey," Rachel assured him.

"How do you know?"

"I don't know," Rachel said. "I just want to believe. It makes me happy."

"Me, too. It makes me real happy," Ben said and hugged her fiercely.

Rachel remembered the conversation as she watched Ben and John eating the homemade soup. Ralph curled up underneath the table near Ben's feet, his tail beating out a regular drum solo of contentment.

Dinner conversation centered on Ben's day at school. He had won a spelling bee and wanted to regale them with a dramatic rendition of the event, spelling each word that had led to his victory. He left the table to retrieve the prize he had won, a blue ribbon with the words "1st PLACE" embossed in gold.

"Ben, that's beautiful," Rachel raved. "What would you like to do with it? Want to put it on the refrigerator so everyone can see it?"

Ben looked at the refrigerator.

"No," he answered.

"How about on the bulletin board in your room?"

Again, Ben mulled over the situation. Then he disappeared under the table. Rachel and John heard whispering for a minute or two. Finally, the child reappeared from under the table, all smiles.

"Ralph wants to wear it. He's sad because he never gets to play in a spelling bee. I want to share the blue ribbon with Ralph." Rachel looked to John to take the lead in a response. He hesitated only a second or two and then pulled Ben up into his lap and nuzzled his neck. Ben giggled. "Granddad, that tickles. Your grizzles are grizzling me."

"You're the grizzle, Ben Turner," John said. "I think your idea is great. Let's finish up our supper. Remember, we've made brownies for dessert. And then we'll figure out a way to attach your blue ribbon to Ralph's collar."

"Ralph's blue ribbon," Ben corrected him. "I want to believe that Ralph is a good speller. I don't know he can spell, but it makes me happy to believe he can spell if he wants to."

Oh dear, I may have started something that can get out of hand here, Rachel thought. Well, it's too late now. "Too late to shut the barn door after the horse is out," she heard her grandmother say.

Too late, indeed.

Chapter Five

L ater that evening, on the third floor in her meditation room, Rachel sat on her zafu, the blue ribbon story jumping from branch to branch in a serious case of monkey mind.

Over and over, she refocused on her breathing. She pulled her shawl around her shoulders like a tight cocoon to protect herself from her own thoughts. Just as she was able to let go of the entertaining thoughts of Ralph and Ben whispering under the table, the worry over what to wear at her wedding jumped out.

Breathe. Breathe.

Then Horace's demand that she take on Carrie's case appeared. Breathe.

Next in line came whether to let John help with the research.

Breathe. Breathe. Breathe.

Rachel couldn't sit still through that one. Monkey mind landed right behind her left ear and pounded. Maybe some tea will help, she thought.

"Come on, Ralph, let's see if we can drown all this mess in some jasmine." Ralph looked doubtful but hopped down from the window seat and padded toward the stairs.

Rachel had just turned on the kitchen light and put the kettle on the stove when she heard a tapping at the back door. She opened it to find Belle standing there in her bathrobe.

"Got a minute?" she asked.

"Sure, come on in. Is Mary asleep?"

"Finally. Can you come downstairs? I don't want to leave her down there alone."

"Sure. I'll bring some tea down with me." Rachel ran upstairs to let John know where she was headed and followed Belle back down the steps to the basement apartment she shared with her daughter.

Rachel marveled at the way Belle had transformed her new home. Cacti lined the sill of the one window in the place. One of them bloomed with red flowers that cascaded over the side of the clay pot, adding a vivid splash to the front of the room. Mary's drawings plastered every empty inch of wall with bright primary Crayola colors. There was only one way to describe the décor: lived and loved in.

Rachel sat down in the old rocking chair Belle had found at a yard sale. On the back, she had spread the one item she had left from her grandmother's possessions. A bright red and green crocheted afghan. Rachel tucked it around her legs and waited to hear what Belle had on her mind. It didn't take long.

"Ricky called," the young woman began. "He wants to see Mary."

Rachel sat for a minute in silence. Scenes of a drunk Ricky's midnight visit flashed across her mental screen. The sight of Ben rushing terrified to the window as the man yelled for Belle from the street below. Of John calling the police and waiting with Belle downstairs. She remembered how long the night had seemed.

She recalled how difficult it had been to talk Belle out of moving. She had felt so guilty for causing problems in the neighborhood. Rachel had filed a restraining order against Ricky, and he hadn't broken it in the months that had passed since the incident.

Now this.

"How did he get your new phone number?" Rachel asked.

"Someone at the shelter must have given it to him, I guess. I stay in touch with Anne down there. She must have thought she was helping."

"How could she possibly think she was helping you by giving Ricky your phone number? And Mary? Why would she want Mary scared again?"

Belle took a sip of tea to buy herself some time.

"He says he's sober. Says he hasn't had a drink in a month, and he's working. He says he wants to make amends."

Right, Rachel thought. How many times have I heard that one before? Thirty days sober, and they want family and friends simply to forget the years and years of neglect or the outright terror of living with a drunk.

But Rachel sipped her tea while she thought about how to respond. Whether to use the lawyer side of her brain and warn Belle to stick by the order the judge had signed to protect her. Or to use the other side of her brain, the one that brought home Ralph, a stray dog with mange.

Belle sat on the edge of the sofa, gripping her teacup like a life preserver. Her bright eyes spoke volumes. Rachel knew what the young woman wanted to hear.

"You gave me a second chance, Rachel. You gave Mary and me a home. Helped us get good medical care when Mary was so sick. Helped me get into school. Maybe now it's time for me to help someone else."

How do I argue with that line of reasoning, Rachel wondered.

"Tell you what," she said. "Why don't you let me sleep on this, and we'll talk about it in the morning."

"What if he calls back tonight?"

"Don't answer the phone."

Sometimes it was best to let the lawyer take charge, Rachel told herself as she let herself in the back door upstairs and locked it securely. John sat at the kitchen table, balancing his checkbook.

"Everything okay downstairs?"

"For right now it is, but I'm afraid a tornado may be headed our way." Rachel sat down at the table across from John and told him about her conversation with Belle. She argued both sides of the debate and then sat back and waited.

John let out a long whistle. "That's a tough one," he said.

"I told her I'd sleep on it, and we'd talk in the morning. Of course, the ultimate decision is Belle's. She's a grown woman, and she's got a mind of her own. I'm flattered that she even asked for my opinion. I think that proves how hard she's trying to turn her life around."

"You've earned her respect, Rachel. Look what you've done for her. Not many people would take in a homeless mother and child they didn't even know."

"Look who's talking. You've trusted her with your grandchild. That's much more than anything I've done."

The two sat silently, thinking of the past few months and what a difference their decisions had made in so many lives. Trusting Belle had proved to be not only a safe gamble but a huge gift. She filled the void left by Ben's mother's death in a way that only a young woman could. And Mary had become a playmate for Ben even though she was so much younger.

"John, the court system is full of cases like this. Understanding, compassionate women who want to give their no-good husbands or boyfriends a second chance. Some of the stories end tragically, I'm afraid."

"How about you and I chaperone when he comes over? Don't let them be alone. We'll be there to make sure he doesn't say or do anything that could possibly hurt them."

"I'm not afraid of that first meeting, John. I'm afraid it will just be the beginning and that down the road sometime, when we're not there, her good intentions will backfire."

John tapped his pencil on the table and frowned.

"I think you're right. This needs some serious sleeping on it."

* * *

When Rachel walked in the kitchen the next morning to make coffee, she found Ralph next to his food bowl, wearing the blue ribbon. He looked very proud of himself.

Rachel laughed. "Well, now aren't you something, Mr. Ralph the spelling bee dog. Can you spell 'coffee,' Ralph? Better yet, can you be trained to MAKE coffee?"

And then Rachel saw that John had beaten her to the job. A couple of cups of coffee were missing from the pot when Rachel poured hers and padded into the den. John sat in the recliner, reading the sports section of the *Washington Post*.

"Looks like you've been up a while," Rachel said, snuggling beside him on the sofa. "You must have had as much trouble sleeping as I did."

"Actually, I didn't. I set my alarm so I could surprise Ben with Ralph in the blue ribbon."

"And me. Thanks. What a great way to start the day."

The two admired Ralph, rubbing his ears and the place right above his tail, his favorite. As if on cue, they looked at each other at the same time. If they had been characters in a cartoon, a light bulb would have been suspended in the air above their heads.

Rachel spoke first. "Ralph looks like a poster with the caption: Homeless dog reformed. Give Ricky a chance."

"It all started with a dog," John said. "So many things do."

Rachel set her coffee cup down and leaned over to throw her arms around John's neck. Their kiss was interrupted by a sleepy voice. "Me, too. Me, too," and Ben leaped into Rachel's lap for a group hug.

When he noticed Ralph wearing his spelling bee prize, he crowed with delight and jumped off the sofa to get a better look. "Can I take him to school with me? Can I, please? I want to show my teacher Ralph's a winner, too."

41

"I don't think dogs are allowed at school, Ben," John said, looking to Rachel for reinforcement as Ben's little face screwed up in a scowl.

"I know what," Rachel said. "How about we take a picture of you and Ralph together, and you can take it to school with you."

Like a light switch had been flipped on, Ben's face brightened.

"Rachel Springer, you are one smart woman," John said.

"And don't you ever forget it, John Turner. You take the picture. I need to get in the shower. I want to run downstairs and talk to Belle before I leave for work. The judge won't think I'm very smart if I'm late for my ten o'clock hearing this morning."

* * *

Belle looked like she'd been handed the keys to the kingdom when Rachel told her that after a good night's rest, she had decided Belle should meet with Ricky. As she watched the young woman's face light up, Rachel hoped the keys wouldn't open the door to hell.

"One thing," Rachel said. "I think you should meet him in a public place and don't take Mary with you. If things turn ugly, you don't want her there. Give him a chance, but take it slow. I wouldn't invite him into your home for a while. Let him prove himself. And, honey, that takes time."

Belle was so relieved to get Rachel's seal of approval that she didn't argue. She hugged her and thanked her for her help.

"He can do this, Rachel. Ricky's a good man at heart."

"You love him, don't you?"

"I know it's hard to believe after what he's done, but I do. At least I think I do."

"I've got to run, but one day real soon you'll have to tell me all about it."

"It's a long story, but I'm ready to share it."

"All stories are long if we live long enough, I guess," Rachel said and kissed her friend on the cheek. "And yours is just beginning."

* * *

Susan watched as Rachel ran up the steps from the basement apartment, just in time to catch a cab passing by. When she looked at an upstairs window, she saw John and Ben inside, getting ready to leave for the day. What a bunch of miracles I've got living across the street from me, she thought. First one thing and then another. Starting with Rachel's move into that house. And then Rachel finding that dog. Everything just lined up. All lined up for such a lovely picture.

Now, if we can just find Rachel a wedding dress, Susan thought as she sat down with a pile of bridal magazines. She raced from page to page, ripping out possibilities and sticking them in a folder labeled "Rachel's dress."

Jim walked in just as she tossed a ragged looking *Modern Bride* toward the trash, narrowly missing his legs.

"Hey, watch it. You almost got me where it hurts," he said, walking over and kissing his wife on the top of her head. "Sorry I won't be home for supper tonight. Got a business dinner, and it'll probably go on pretty late. Don't wait up for me."

Susan flipped another page a little more viciously than the last. "Same client as last week?"

"Yeah. Very demanding, but all this wining and dining will pay off, I'm sure. Big project and a lot of firms trying to get it. Sorry I can't take you with me, but you'd be bored to death. Why don't you call Rachel and see if she'd like to go to a movie with you?"

"Rachel's got a family now, Jim," Susan said. She slammed the magazine shut and threw it on the floor. "She doesn't have time to baby-sit me every time you're gone." Which seems to be more and more often, she resisted saying.

Jim patted her arm, grabbed his briefcase and dashed out the door, tossing a "love you" over his shoulder.

"Do you really?" Susan whispered as she crossed to the window to watch her husband walk briskly down the sidewalk toward the metro station.

Jim was still a good-looking man at 60 years old. He began shaving his head when he started to lose his hair. Susan found the new look sexy and told him so. He kept in shape playing racket ball and golf. His closet looked like an ad for Polo Ralph Lauren. Susan teased him that he spent more money on clothes than she did. Shoes were a real weakness for him, and he had a different pair of golf shoes for each day of the week. He said they were his secret weapon on the course.

Today he was wearing the penny loafers Susan had shined for him the night before. She wondered if he had noticed the new pennies she had stuck in.

"Oh, Jim," she whispered to herself as he disappeared around the corner. "I miss you so much."

Jim and Susan had met at the University of Virginia in their freshman year. Much to their parents' horror and against their collective advice, the two had gotten married in the summer after their sophomore year. The first baby was born nine months after they graduated.

"What a wonderful graduation present," Susan had proclaimed from her hospital bed. Her father had grumbled about all the money he had wasted on her education. Her mother had insisted every penny was worth spending because Susan had found such a suitable husband. A clean-cut young man from a "good family" and on a good career path as an engineer.

Susan had never worked. Jim made enough money to support her and their two children. Throughout her marriage, she had consistently maintained that she found being a fulltime wife and mother totally satisfying. When her second child entered first grade, she found a book club and a garden club to fill her spare time. Over the years, she had taken classes in watercolors, tap dancing and weaving. She volunteered at the hospital and the battered women's shelter. From time to time, she audited a class at Georgetown University to keep her brain sharp.

As Susan picked up the scattered magazines, she wondered why she felt such a gaping hole lately. Surely, she wasn't jealous of Rachel. While she enjoyed her time with Ben whenever she was asked to baby-sit, the last thing she wanted was to have a child living with her fulltime. She had plenty of energy to live an active 60-something lifestyle, but in her opinion, that did not include rearing a child.

She complained that she didn't see her own grandchildren often enough, but she certainly didn't want anything to happen to their parents so they'd have to come live with her. The thought that she might have to do what John Turner had done when Ben's parents were killed sent cold chills down her spine.

And she didn't envy Rachel's late-in-life romance. As exciting as those first few months of a relationship could be, Susan wouldn't trade them for the comfortable-old-shoe feeling she had with Jim.

At least until recently. Until Jim's new client required so much of his time. The new "potential client," she corrected herself. The one everyone in town was trying to get. Poor Jim. He must be under a lot of stress. I'll have to try to be more understanding, Susan chided herself. Maybe I'll call to see if I can take him to lunch. Somewhere relaxing. Or maybe a picnic basket of some of his favorite foods, and we can spread a blanket on his office floor like we used to when he first got the job.

Susan jumped up and began making a list of what she needed to buy. Within minutes she was off to the market.

Chapter Six

B elle kissed her daughter good-bye and walked out Mrs. Moser's back door. When she looked back, Mary and her elderly neighbor were sitting on the kitchen floor, cutting paper dolls out of an old Sears Roebuck catalog. Belle marveled at the change in her relationship with the old woman. She knew that Mrs. Moser thought Rachel had made a serious mistake by inviting the homeless family into her house. The old woman had made no effort to hide her feelings of distrust.

Mrs. Moser and Belle's grandmother had been friends for years, and she held Belle responsible for her grandmother's death. She said she had broken the old woman's heart with worry about her life on the streets. In fact, one day shortly after Belle's move, Mrs. Moser had confronted her.

"You should be ashamed of yourself, living the way you did," the old woman had said. "Living on the streets with that bum. You might as well have stuck a knife in your grandmother's heart."

Mary had been the one to win her neighbor over, softening the old woman's heart with her childlike innocence. The Moser's had no children of their own, and they doted on Mary and Ben. But especially Mary. Not a day went by that the child didn't spend at least a little time with her adopted grandparents, helping Mrs. Moser in her flower garden or baking cookies. Mrs. Moser loved to teach her the names of all the different birds that frequented the many feeders hanging around the yard.

"I knew I'd find a good use for these old catalogs," Mrs. Moser said as she started cutting out pictures of models and furniture for a paper house she and Mary would set up under the kitchen table. Belle smiled at the image of the little old lady and the tiny girl huddled on the floor, playing house.

Ricky was waiting for her near Deejee's hot dog stand where they had agreed to meet. Belle hadn't seen him since the night he'd been arrested in front of Rachel's house. If she hadn't agreed to meet him at that spot, she didn't think she would have recognized him. He had cut his hair and shaved the long, straggly beard. He wore what looked like a pair of new chinos and a clean white shirt.

But it was his eyes that made the most startling difference. They were clear and shone with a light Belle had never seen. Rather than focusing on anything other than the woman he had hurt, he looked directly at her and smiled.

"Ricky?"

"Morning, Belle. You sure look pretty this morning." Ricky stood at a respectful distance. He knew not to push his luck. He waited.

"You look good, too." Belle stared, taking in the transformation. She was afraid to acknowledge the change, afraid that if she mentioned it, the new Ricky would suddenly disappear.

"Want to sit down? Can I get you a hot dog? Something to drink? A Coke, maybe?" Ricky pulled out a new leather wallet, and Belle could see a ten dollar bill tucked neatly inside.

"A Coke would be good. Yes, thank you. A Coke." Belle felt her heart race. "Careful," she could hear Rachel say. This is probably a trick. Don't let him get too close. She watched Ricky walk with purpose over to the hot dog vendor. He chatted with Deejee while she took two cans of Coke out of her cooler and made change. Belle was encouraged by the smile on Deejee's face. Ricky had never been one of the vendor's favorites in the little homeless community that gathered at the Circle.

Even Chelsea, the teenager with the punk purple hair, smiled at him as he passed by her bench on the way back to where Belle sat. Ricky stopped to chat, and Belle watched as the girl's face became more animated than she could remember ever seeing it.

Belle remembered Chelsea's fierce conviction that Ricky had been responsible for Ralph's disappearance months ago. She had been sure that he had kidnapped the dog out of revenge after Rachel filed a temporary restraining order. Obviously, the girl's opinion of Ricky had changed. Belle watched as he gave the homeless girl a handful of coins.

"That girl needs to go home to her folks and make some amends," Ricky said as he sat down on the bench beside Belle. "But she's just not ready, I guess. Can't do nothing . . . Can't do ANYTHING until you're ready. Trying to work on my grammar. Guess I've got enough of my own problems to work on without trying to fix hers. Sorry about that."

Belle was still too shocked by what she was seeing to say anything at all. Ricky popped the tab on one Coke can and handed it to her. "Cheers," he said and gently tapped his can against hers.

"Cheers," Belle said.

Ricky sat silently. The legs Belle remembered always twitching and jerking lay still. He sipped the drink and sat. Belle felt her own body relax. This isn't too bad, she thought. I can do this.

Ricky seemed to know intuitively that the quiet – the simple act of sitting – was necessary, and so he sat. They watched the pigeons and the city traffic. A church bell rang in the distance. A bus horn blasted at a taxi that cut in front of it. Ricky sat at the opposite end of the bench, but, even at a distance, Belle could hear his steady breathing. The rasp was missing, she realized. And he smelled good.

"You quit smoking?" she asked.

"Two weeks ago. It's been harder than giving up the booze and the drugs. Cigarettes are a real bitch. Oh, sorry. Can't seem to quit the cussing."

Belle laughed. The two looked at each other. Belle couldn't remember the last time they had laughed together.

"Belle, I need to say some things to you. You don't need to say anything back. All you need to do is listen, but I'd sure appreciate it if you would. Are you willing to just listen to me?"

"Guess I wouldn't be here if I wasn't willing, would I?"

"Well, I guess not," Ricky said. He got up from the bench and sat on the ground in front of her so he faced her. "Remember when we first met?" he began.

Belle nodded but didn't say anything. She felt her chest constrict at the memory.

"You were wearing those black bib overalls with a pink bikini top under them. You were flying a kite up on the Washington Monument hill. I thought I'd never seen anything as cute as you in my life. I fell in love with you right there on the spot."

"I've still got those bibs somewhere. Can't wear them anymore. Got a hole in the bottom where I finally sat down in them one too many times."

Ricky smiled. "Maybe I could patch them for you."

Belle looked away. This new Ricky – this earnest young man so eager to help – made her squirm. Her palms felt wet as she reached up to push back a strand of loose hair. She wondered what had happened to that kite. What had happened to the young girl flying it?

Ricky watched her, giving her time to feel whatever she felt. He watched her emotions pass over her face like clouds. He waited for the sun. When it failed to appear, he reached out to touch her hand.

"Belle, I'm sorry for everything I did since then to hurt you." When she didn't look at him, he went on. At least she didn't pull her hand away, he thought. "I'm sorry I hurt you, but I'm even sorrier I hurt Mary. I hate what I did to you, putting you in danger by living on the streets. Putting my need for crack ahead of everything. Living in a car ain't – isn't the life you and she deserve. I can't believe I dragged the person – the people I loved the most in my whole life down in the gutter with me." Tears ran down Ricky's face as he spoke.

"Don't be too hard on yourself, Ricky. I was as much to blame as you were. I was doing drugs right along with you."

"But you never would have started if I hadn't come along. You'd never even smoked pot before you met me."

"I was an adult, Ricky. I had a choice." Belle rose from the bench and walked a few feet away. A pigeon bobbed its head up and down, pecking at some crumbs scattered on the ground near her feet.

When she looked back at Ricky, he still crouched on the ground, waiting patiently. He had aged so much since that day at the monument. She wondered where the guitar was he had played for her that day.

Ricky had been the bass player in a band. Belle had fit easily into the small collection of groupies that followed the musicians around the DC area as they played at some small club almost every night. The late hours took their toll, and she traded school for the more exciting life with a would-be rock star.

And then the drugs started to rob Ricky of his music and he, too, became a drop-out. The other members of the group grew tired of him being late for gigs or not showing up at all. The time he and Belle both arrived on stage high as the long lost kite, the band's leader told him to leave and not to come back.

With all income gone, it wasn't long before they were kicked out of their apartment and living in their car. Then, Belle discovered she was pregnant.

"Can you forgive me, Belle Mason? Can you find it in your heart ever to forgive what I've done to you and Mary? I'm not asking you to forget. I'm not even asking you to give me another chance yet. But can you forgive me?"

"What does that mean, Ricky? To forgive? I don't even know. My family didn't forgive. I never learned. They knew how to make money. They knew how to ride horses and throw fancy parties. Forgive wasn't part of their repertoire."

Belle's voice rose as she raced through her pain. Her parents had turned their backs on her when she dropped out of school and moved in with Ricky. Even her grandmother had disowned her. The day Belle met Rachel and learned that she had bought her grandmother's house from the old woman's estate was the first time she had been in the house in years. The sight of the banister she slid down as a child brought back a torrent of memories that were almost more than she could handle at the time.

During the months since she moved into Rachel's downstairs apartment, she had felt a growing connection with her grandmother again. A healing had begun. Forgiveness? Maybe some of that was what was going on. Belle wasn't sure.

Ricky sensed her hesitation. He got up from the ground and stood, giving her space. "All I asked was for you to listen, Belle. You did." He stepped forward and handed her a piece of paper. On it was a phone number. "That's the law firm where I work. Call me, please. Call me when we can meet again."

"You're working for a lawyer?"

"Yeah. He's my AA sponsor. It's a hole-in-the-wall office up three flights of stairs in the back of an old warehouse, but he pays me," Ricky laughed. "And he's a good guy. I'd like for you to meet him some day."

Belle didn't answer but she didn't say "no" either. "I've got to go, Ricky. Mrs. Moser has Mary, and I don't like to leave her there too long. The woman's getting old, and she tires quickly."

"Mary doing okay?"

"She's fine."

Ricky reached in his pocket and pulled out a twenty-dollar bill and held it out toward Belle. "Here," he said. "I've been saving so I could give you this."

Belle hesitated, torn between her fear of giving Ricky any reason for hope and her need for money. The mother's instinctive need to protect her child won, and she took the money.

"Thanks," she said without looking up.

"No, thank YOU, Belle. Thanks for listening."

Belle felt a tingle as their hands touched. She looked up, and their eyes held each other.

"Gotta go," Belle said and rushed off before she weakened and let him hug her. She knew that's what he wanted, but she wasn't quite ready. When she reached the corner, she turned to look back and saw Deejee doing what she couldn't. The woman's arms wrapped around Ricky, and Belle wasn't sure, but she thought she saw his shoulders shaking.

The light changed, the traffic stopped and Belle crossed the street to the other side.

* * *

Susan's mouth fell open when she saw a new face behind the receptionist's desk in Jim's office. The face was young, pretty and heavily made-up, a far cry from Ethel Jefferson, who had manned the front office for the past 15 years.

"Good morning," the young woman chirped. "May I help you?" She eyed Susan's picnic basket and bottle of wine suspiciously.

"Good morning. Where's Ethel?"

"Mrs. Jefferson is out on medical leave. I'm Betty Lou. And you are?"

Susan dropped the picnic basket on the floor and set the bottle of wine down carefully on the desk, holding out her hand. "I'm Jim's wife. My name is Susan."

Betty Lou jumped up and took Susan's hand, shaking it a little too enthusiastically, Susan thought.

"Nice to meet you. I'll tell Jim you're here."

"Oh, that won't be necessary. I know where his office is," Susan said. She grabbed the wine and the basket and marched down the hall. "Unless there's something else he hasn't told me and he's got a new office, too," she muttered under her breath.

Jim's office door sat open, and he sat with his back to the hallway, talking on the phone as Susan walked in. The sound of the door shutting caused him to swivel in his chair.

"Gotta go," he said to the person on the other end. "Talk to you tomorrow." Jim hung up the phone and leaned across the desk to peck Susan on the cheek. "What a surprise. What you got there?"

Susan spread an old Army blanket on the floor and opened up the basket. She pulled out a corkscrew and went to work opening the bottle of wine. She still hadn't spoken.

"What's this all about?" Jim asked, sounding none too pleased by the interruption to his day.

"I just thought you'd appreciate a little treat. You've been working such long hours lately. We used to do this a lot when you first started working here. Remember how much fun we had? Come on, Jim, take a break."

Susan poured two glasses of white wine, careful not to spill any on Jim's expensive Oriental rug. Jim looked at his watch and then at the closed door. "Well, I guess I can take a few minutes." He looked at his calendar and picked up the phone and punched a button. "Betty Lou, do me a favor and call my one o'clock and tell them I'll be a little late. Thanks."

Jim walked around the desk and dropped down to the floor near his wife.

"So, where did you find Betty Lou and what's wrong with Ethel? You didn't tell me she was sick."

Jim took a sip of wine and a bite of cheese. "You sure I didn't tell you? I thought I told you last week. She had to have a hysterectomy. She may not come back, in fact. She may take an early retirement."

Susan watched as her husband searched through the basket for a napkin, found one and then made an elaborate production of tucking it in the neck of his starched white shirt and spreading it carefully so that not an inch of cloth was exposed.

Susan served them both wedges of spanakopita and grapes. "Save some room for dessert," she said. "I bought cannolis. Your favorite."

Jim closed his eyes and groaned with pleasure.

"So, where did you find Betty Lou? She's very pretty. Can she type?"

"Got her through the temp agency Rachel uses."

"You mean Rachel knew about Ethel, and she didn't tell me either?"

"No, Rachel didn't know. I remembered her mentioning the name of the agency. Gee, Susan, what's wrong with you? Why are you making such a big deal about this?"

"I'm not making a big deal about anything. I just . . ." Susan stopped before the words "feel so left out" escaped her lips. Maybe she was being crazy. She heard her father's voice saying, "buck up, little lady." And she tried.

"So, I think I've got a plan for how to solve Rachel's wedding dress dilemma," she said, changing the subject so abruptly that Jim's eyes rolled toward the ceiling as he poured more wine. "I'm going to find a museum that displays wedding dresses somewhere in the city and take her to see them. Surely, that will inspire her, don't you think?"

Jim stared out the window.

"Jim, have you been listening to a word I've said?"

Jim jerked his head back in her direction. "Susan, I think that's a great idea. You've always got great ideas."

Susan smiled and leaned across to her husband. "I've got another great idea. How about we lock the door like we used to and . . ." She licked his ear.

Jim's eyebrows arched, and he pulled away from her. "Susan, are you out of your mind? We're not nutty kids anymore. We're —"

A knock at the door interrupted him. He jumped up and rushed over to open it.

"Sorry, Jim," Betty Lou said. "Just wanted to let you know I'm leaving for lunch." She peered around Jim to get a look at Susan, sitting with the picnic lunch on the floor. She stepped in to get a better look and then turned on her stiletto heels and walked away.

"What was that all about?" Susan asked.

"God only knows," Jim said, stooping down to put the remains of lunch back in the basket. "Hey, listen, Susan, thanks for doing this. You're sweet to worry about me, but you really shouldn't. I'm fine."

Well, I'm not, Susan thought, but the "buck up" message stopped her from speaking.

"Now, I hate to do this, but I really do have a meeting to prepare for, so if you don't mind —"

Susan stood up and brushed the crumbs from her pants into the trash. "Sure, honey, I understand. See you around six?"

"I think I'll be home by then. Maybe we can take in a movie or something." Jim gave her a hug and almost pushed her out the door in his rush to get on with his afternoon.

As Susan walked by the receptionist's desk, she noticed a vase with a single yellow rose. She stopped and took a closer look. She set down the picnic basket and walked back to Jim's office.

"Jim?"

Jim looked up from the briefcase into which he was furiously stuffing papers and file folders. "What now?" he asked with some irritation.

55

"Is that one of our silver bud vases on Betty Lou's desk?"

At first, Jim looked like he was going to deny the fact, but then he seemed to have second thoughts. "Yeah, today's her birthday, and we didn't have anything to put a single rose in. I'll be sure to bring it home when she's done with it."

"Yes, please do," Susan said. "When she's done with it. Bring it home."

The vase was one Jim had given her on their 10th wedding anniversary. Something silver. It looked like it had been newly polished, Susan thought as she walked back to the desk.

Susan took the rose out of the vase, poured the water into the empty wine bottle and stuck the rose down in it. "Happy birthday, Betty Lou," she muttered as she walked out of the office.

Chapter Seven

W hat have you decided to do about Carrie Johnson?" Georgia asked Rachel. "You gonna take the case? She called this morning to find out."

Rachel eased herself into the rocking chair that faced her secretary's desk. She rocked and pondered. Ralph jumped down from his seat in the window and walked over to lick her hand as if he knew she needed some help making the decision.

"I don't know, Georgia. What do you think?"

Georgia took a sip of coffee and peered at her boss over the cup's rim. They'd worked together for a long time and rarely had she seen Rachel struggle over a decision about whether to take on a new client. She had always made the choice easily and with no doubts to delay the process.

"Well, I haven't seen the notebooks," Georgia said, "since John's had them. I don't know much about the invention."

"That's part of the problem, Georgia."

"What? I don't know what you're talking about."

Rachel rubbed Ralph in his sweet spot and considered whether to expose the underbelly of her fear. Being in love was such a new emotion for her, and she wasn't always sure whether she should share some of her uglier feelings.

She looked at Georgia, sitting behind her desk, patiently waiting. Finally, she decided help was more important than protecting her image.

"I'm not sure it would be a good idea for John and me to work together," she said. "Things are going so well between us and I just don't want to rock the boat by putting him in a position where he has to think of me as his boss."

"How about making him your partner instead of a subordinate? Wouldn't that work?"

Rachel gave the idea a minute to sink in. It didn't take long for her to remember the disastrous relationship advice Susan had given her not too long ago.

George, her cousin's farm manager, had announced that he was coming to DC to visit friends and asked Rachel to go to dinner with him while he was in town. Susan had suggested that she accept the invitation, saying that a little jealousy would add some spice to Rachel's relationship with John.

The spice had been too hot for John, however, and she almost lost him.

"I don't know, Georgia. I'll have to think about it some more."

"I hate to see you torture yourself over something that's not really that big a deal, Rachel. Loosen up. You're not going to be able to avoid all problems, you know. And you'll survive them. Plus, if you wait too long to let this woman know something, she'll find somebody else to do the work."

Rachel smiled and walked into her office. Georgia trailed behind her.

"Rachel Springer," she said, sounding just like Rachel's grandmother, "you're hoping she'll go to another law firm, aren't you?"

When Rachel didn't answer, Georgia forged ahead.

"This is not like you. Passive aggressive isn't your style. What's wrong with you? I'm not leaving this office until you tell me," she said and sat down in the chair nearest Rachel's desk. When the phone rang and she didn't answer it, Rachel knew her secretary was making a serious stand. Experience told her that Georgia was not to be diverted from her mission.

"Nothing's wrong with me, Georgia. Nothing serious, that is."

"Then what's wrong with you that's not serious?"

Ralph inched into the room, tail between his legs and ears flattened as though he sensed trouble.

"Okay, I'm scared. This whole wedding thing has me crazy. I'm just not sure I'm ready."

Georgia laughed. "You were ready to move the guy into your basement. You were ready to move him and a child upstairs to live in your space. You weren't afraid to invite a homeless family into your house, but you're spooked by something thousands of people do every day. Now you tell me, does that make sense?"

Rachel sat, silently, looking like a little girl who can't work up the nerve to climb the ladder to the sliding board. All the rest of the children are standing behind her, yelling to her to climb.

"Rachel, have you been meditating?"

"Yes. Well, sort of . . . "

"Have you been exercising?"

Silence.

"Maybe you need a massage. Here, let me make you an emergency appointment," Georgia said and rushed out to her desk to make the call.

"Georgia," Rachel called, but her cry went unanswered. Within minutes, Georgia was back with a piece of paper in her hand. "There, you've got a three o'clock appointment with Elizabeth. I'll cancel the rest of your appointments for the afternoon."

"Thanks, Georgia."

"And tomorrow, we'll call Carrie Johnson and give her your decision. Come on, Ralph, time to go outside."

Rachel watched as woman and dog disappeared out the front door, leaving her to deal with her demons alone.

* * *

When Susan described her idea to make a "wedding gown tour," Rachel wasn't sure she'd heard right. In the few seconds it took her to respond, Susan launched into her second attack.

"Come on, Rachel, it'll be so much fun. We'll look at the dresses, you'll get inspired, we'll have lunch and then we'll go buy a dress. We'll make a whole day of it."

"Susan, stop. I really don't have time for this. I'm not going to get inspired by a collection of couture gowns behind glass. I know it. No doubt."

Then she waited for Susan's next attack. When the follow-up didn't come, and Susan appeared to have backed off in a way she had never done as long as Rachel had known her, Rachel felt surprise. Then she heard Susan crying on the other end of the phone line.

"Susan, are you all right?"

"No, Rachel, I'm not," Susan wailed and hung up the phone.

Rachel sat, holding the phone in her hand for a few minutes. She had never known this side of her friend. Had never, in fact, seen her cry. She placed the receiver back in its cradle and looked at Ralph.

"Come on, boy. We're needed across the street."

Rachel called up the stairs to John and Ben to tell them that she needed to run across the street to see Susan for a minute, but that she'd be back in time for supper.

When she found Susan's front door locked, she walked around to the back and let herself in through the kitchen. Her friend wasn't anywhere on the first floor. Rachel called her name. No answering call came, so she climbed the stairs to the second floor where she found Susan stretched out across her four-poster bed. She lay buried under a quilt. Only her feet were visible, sticking out from one end of the patchwork that covered her. The mound heaved with Susan's sobs.

"My god, Susan, what in the world is wrong?" Rachel rushed to her friend and pulled her out of her cocoon. "Listen, I'll go with you to look at gowns. Good Lord, I had no idea this meant so much to you. I'll go. When do you want to do it? Tomorrow? I can . . ."

"Stop Rachel," Susan moaned, wiping her face with a corner of the quilt. "Stop. It's not that."

"Then what is it, Susan? I've never seen you like this. Tell me quick. Are you sick? Is Jim sick?"

Susan rose from the bed and padded into the master bathroom. Rachel heard her friend blow her nose a couple of times. She heard the sound of water running as she washed her face. When she walked back into the bedroom, her wrinkled pajamas rattled Rachel.

"Yeah, I know," Susan said. "I look like a wreck. Sorry."

Rachel reached out to pat her friend's shoulder. She waited as Susan propped herself up on the mountain of pillows at the head of the bed and looked at Rachel.

"Jim's having an affair," she announced, her voice falling like a bomb into the bedroom she had shared with her husband for most of their married life.

Rachel felt the hit and couldn't find her voice. How many times had she sat across her desk and heard these same words. She knew all the questions she was supposed to ask but somehow none of them seemed appropriate when the wronged wife was her best friend.

"Oh, Susan. I'm so sorry. Are you sure?"

Susan nodded.

Rachel waited for the story to unfold. When it didn't, she let her mind play with all kinds of possibilities as she simply sat with her friend's misery. Finally she managed to ask the one question that seemed the most important at the time.

"Have you two talked about it?"

"No."

"Well, what makes you think he's having an affair?"

Susan reached under the mattress and pulled out a slip of paper and handed it to Rachel. The receipt from a local motel. "I found it in one of his jacket pockets this morning," Susan managed to say before she dissolved into another fit of weeping.

Rachel glanced at the receipt for one night's stay at the Bluebird Motel and laid it carefully on the bedside table. She sat on the side of the bed with her hand resting on Susan's heaving back. When the sobbing subsided again, she suggested they move downstairs for some tea. Susan reluctantly agreed.

Rachel left her friend to collect herself and ran downstairs to put the kettle of water on the stove. She looked around the kitchen at all the memorabilia of a 40-year marriage. Refrigerator magnets brought back from family trips. Pictures of Jim and Susan at parties. Children. Grandchildren.

Jim's golf bag sat at the back door with the pair of golf shoes he had most recently worn. He had probably left them there for Susan to clean for him, Rachel thought. If he walked through the door right now, I'd probably hit him over the head with one of those clubs, Rachel thought.

Jim might actually walk through the door at any moment and I'll be caught in the middle of a scene no married couple wants to share, even with their best friend, she realized.

Rachel climbed the stairs to see what was taking Susan so long. She found her washing her face again.

"Susan, are you expecting Jim for supper?"

Susan nodded. Rachel looked at her watch. "What time did he say he'd be home?"

"Seven."

Rachel breathed a sigh of relief. It was only 5:30. She had plenty of time to pour tea for Susan, talk things over and retreat back across the street before the fireworks started.

Looking at Susan though, she didn't see fireworks material. She saw a sinking ship, and it was going under fast.

"Come on, honey, your tea is getting cold." Rachel took Susan's hand and led her across the hall and down the backstairs to the kitchen. She eased her down in one of the kitchen chairs and poured her a cup of steaming jasmine tea. Susan sat staring at it, frozen.

"Go ahead now, take a sip. It'll make you feel better."

Susan lifted the cup like a feeble old woman and brought it to her mouth. Midway to its destination, she set it back down as though she had forgotten what she was doing.

Rachel wrestled with whether she would help her friend more by sitting with her in silence, sharing her pain, or whether she should take a more practical approach and dive into the problem and try to come up with a solution.

Compromising, she sat for about five minutes of silence and then dived in. "Susan, you've got to talk to Jim. This may not be what it appears. Maybe you're torturing yourself needlessly."

Susan looked at her friend out of eyes that had lost all their light. As though the hidden receipt from the Bluebird Motel had doused the light in one tragic moment.

"There's more," Susan whispered. "He's been coming home late a lot."

Rachel waited.

"He doesn't kiss me anymore, Rachel. REALLY kiss me. He PECKS me."

Rachel was glad to see some anger light up the eyes, at least. Susan revived enough to take a sip of tea.

"And Ethel's gone."

Rachel waited for an explanation as to why Jim's elderly receptionist being gone had anything to do with the motel receipt.

"So?"

"So, he's got Betty Lou now. Young, pretty Betty Lou. I think she's the one he's having an affair with."

Rachel's mouth dropped open but nothing came out. Finally, she closed it and tried to gather her thoughts.

"Okay, now, Susan, I've known Jim for a long time, and I can't imagine him trading you for a receptionist named Betty Lou."

Susan laid her head on the table and began to weep again. Rachel moved the teacup that was on the verge of being upset by Susan's sudden collapse. As she stood up to take the cup and saucer to the sink, the back door opened, and Jim walked in.

Rachel almost dropped everything she was holding. "You're early," she stammered.

Before he could respond, Jim saw Susan and stopped. "What's going on?" he asked.

"You tell me, Jim," Rachel couldn't restrain herself from asking. She had hoped to avoid the scene by being safely across the street when Jim got home, but since she found herself thrust unwillingly into the middle of it, she felt duty-bound to play the role of her friend's protector.

Susan hadn't even raised her head from the table at the sound of Jim's voice. He looked at Rachel as though he were standing on another planet, looking at aliens rather than in his own kitchen with two women he knew as well as he knew himself.

Rachel waited for Susan to take over in her usual takeover way. When she didn't, Rachel went upstairs to retrieve the motel receipt. When she came back into the room less than two minutes later, Jim was kneeling on the floor beside Susan's chair. He had poured her a glass of water and was trying to offer her a drink.

Rachel handed him the motel receipt. "Susan found this in your jacket pocket. She thinks you're having an affair," she said.

Jim slammed the glass down on the table. Some of the water splashed onto Susan's pajama sleeve, jolting her upright. At the sight of her red, blotchy face, Jim took a step backwards. He dropped into the chair across the table from his wife.

64

The only sounds in the kitchen were the tick of the clock and the hum of the refrigerator. Rachel was the first to speak. "Well, are you?" she asked. "Are you cheating on your wife?"

Jim aimed all his wrath at Rachel. "I am not. I have never, and am not now, cheating on Susan, and anyone who thinks I am doesn't really know me very well."

Jim shook the receipt in Rachel's face, unable to bring himself to acknowledge the person he felt most intensely hurt by. "This receipt is for reimbursement for the room our new client stayed in. The one I've been working so hard lately to bring on board."

Finally, he turned to face Susan. Tears filled his eyes, but he brushed them away before they were able to fall. "Susan, how could you think that of me?"

Rachel didn't know whether she should stay or leave the two alone. The moment deserved privacy, but her friend looked so vulnerable. The phone rang, and she picked it up out of habit.

"Hey, when are you coming home?" John asked. "Supper's getting cold."

"Be right there," Rachel said and hung up. "That was John," she said. "You guys probably want to be alone. I'll be across the street if you need me." Rachel hugged Susan. She wasn't sure what to do with Jim but managed a weak smile on her way out the door. She closed it gently.

Susan looked across the table at her husband, holding the motel receipt. They sat in silence. Finally, Jim got up and went over to the cabinet above the stove and took out a bottle of Scotch. He poured alcohol into a cocktail glass. "Want some?" he asked.

Susan shook her head, too drained to answer. Fortified, Jim walked back to where she sat at the table, looking like a deflated balloon in her pink pajamas.

"I don't remember every seeing you in pj's at this time of day," he said. "Not your best look, I might add."

When Susan didn't respond, Jim thought better of his wisecrack and apologized. But he didn't know another approach to a situation that had caught him so off-guard. He knew he felt wounded by the accusation, but it was such an unfamiliar feeling that he didn't know what to do with it. Susan was obviously in no shape, herself, to hear how hurt he felt. He had known her for a long time and he'd never seen her look so defeated. To share his own sense of betrayal seemed cruel. So he stuffed it and poured another shot of Dewar's. He felt the welcome numbness descend.

"Come on, Susan, why don't you take a shower and get dressed. We'll go out to eat. Somewhere nice. Your pick. Where do you want to go?"

Susan finally looked into Jim's eyes. She saw the pain beyond the Scotch and realized that her doubts had been as damaging to her marriage as another woman could have been.

"Let's order Chinese," she said and left the room to take a shower.

Chapter Eight

John and Ben sat at the kitchen table, eating meatloaf and mashed potatoes when Rachel walked in the back door. The smell of homemade biscuits filled the air.

"Quick, Rachel, sit down before the biscuits get cold," Ben squealed. "We made them specially for you." The child reached into the basket. "Here's yours," he said, pulling out a lumpy ball, smaller than the rest. Rachel took a bite and pronounced it the best biscuit she had ever tasted.

"What's going on across the street?" John asked. "You looked like you'd come from the scene of a wreck when you walked in. Glad we had biscuits waiting for you."

"I feel like I've witnessed a wreck. Thanks for supper. It's helping."

John waited for the story. He knew not to push. Rachel would tell him when she was ready. Or not.

After the dishes were loaded into the dishwasher and Ben tucked in bed, she and John settled into their usual spots in the den. He had made a fire and the two sat companionably together on the sofa, listening to the logs crackle. The flames cast dancing shadows on the walls. As he held her hand, John could feel Rachel's tension.

"Want to talk about it?" he nudged, turning so he could see Rachel's eyes. She huddled in silence for so long he had almost decided she wasn't going to say anything. Then she spoke.

She told him about Susan finding the motel receipt and about Jim's denial that it was his.

"I'm afraid the damage has been done though, even if he's telling the truth," she said. "Jim looked so wounded by the fact that Susan didn't trust him. And getting caught in the middle of their pain was one of the worst things I've ever experienced. And I've seen a lot of wounded wives in my career."

"Are you sure he's telling the truth?" John asked.

"Seems like it." Rachel's brow furrowed as she worked through the dilemma in her mind. "Only he knows."

John took her face in his hands and kissed her lips gently. He kissed her a second time, but she still didn't respond.

"Rachel, what is it?"

"Guess I'm just a little shook by this, John. I know it's not about me, but somehow I feel completely drained. Think I'll go on to bed. Thanks for supper. The biscuits were great."

Rachel stood up and patted John on the shoulder as she walked out of the room and up the stairs. As she closed her door, she heard John downstairs, laying another log on the fire.

* * *

The skies still hung darkly around the house when Ralph pulled at Rachel's braid, rousing her from a deep and yet troubled sleep. Off and on, all night, she had dreamed the same scene that had chased her nights for as long as she could remember.

She sat on a horse, a giant horse, taller than a horse could possibly be. Black with huge, flaring nostrils. How she had managed to mount it remained a mystery never solved during the many years the dream had reoccurred. She never saw herself get on or off the animal.

She rode the horse bareback. He glided gently across the wide expanse of her dreams, never galloping or leaping. She never felt afraid. Nobody else was ever in the dream, just her and the horse, traveling. Sometimes across mountains, sometimes beside a wide expanse of ocean. Once, recently, along the edge of a gaping canyon which she felt the horse wanted to cross. In the dream, Rachel was able to restrain him by whispering into his ear words she could not hear.

Ralph's tugging at her hair persisted.

"What is it? It's not time to get up. Leave me alone," she moaned from under the quilt she had pulled over her head during the night.

When Ralph persisted, adding a soft whine for emphasis, Rachel threw back the covers. The dog, confident that she was sufficiently awake, ran toward the closed door and waited.

For some reason, known only to him, Ralph had insisted on sleeping at the foot of her bed that night instead of his usual place in Ben's room. He had waited until the boy was asleep and then crept in to curl up beside her in the den. He had followed her upstairs when she said good-night to John.

Rachel padded over to the door and opened it. Ralph rushed down the hall to the door to Ben's room, where Rachel saw the boy standing, rubbing his eyes.

"I couldn't find Ralph, and I called his name, but he didn't come," the child cried.

"I didn't hear you call," Rachel said. "Ralph has good ears."

Ben wrinkled his nose, squinted his eyes and pulled at his hair. "What was he doing in your room? He sleeps with me."

"I don't know. Do you want him with you? We can share. There's still some night left."

Ben seemed to study the situation seriously. Then his face lit up.

"I know what," he said. "He can sleep with both of us," and he ran down the hall and hopped into Rachel's bed. Too sleepy to think better of the problems that might be created by setting such a precedent, Rachel crawled into the warmth of her bed beside him.

Ralph flopped down on the floor next to them.

As she drifted off to sleep again, she heard a little voice from the other pillow. "Poor Granddad. He's all alone."

Rachel pretended to be asleep. Within minutes, a soft snore assured her that Ben had fallen back to sleep, too.

* * *

A few hours later, she was awakened by John's voice. Sunshine streamed through the windows of her bedroom, casting a golden light across the mound of covers around dog and boy.

"What is this all about?" John asked, peering around the edge of the door. "Was there a pajama party last night I didn't get invited to?"

Ben leaped out of bed and into his grandfather's arms, wrapping him in a fierce hug. "I tried to get Rachel to let you come, too, but she was already asleep."

Rachel opened one eye to gauge John's reaction. He was already dressed and looked ready for the day. She remembered that they had decided to take Ben for a ride on the C&O Canal barge. As she rolled onto her back, she wondered if she had the energy. Last night's scene across the street had drained her. She felt 20 years older than when she had collapsed into bed only hours before.

"Come on, Ben, let's give Rachel some privacy."

"Why does she need pribacy?"

"Well, let's give her space to wake up quietly. How about that? Come on downstairs with me. We'll let Ralph outside."

The magic word "Ralph" did the trick. Ben bounded out the door, dog trailing behind him. John walked over and tugged Rachel's braid. "You forgot to undo your hair. Must be bad," he said and kissed her on the top of her head. "Would you like me to bring you a cup of coffee in bed?"

"And the Post?"

"And the Post."

"Do we have enough time? We told Ben we'd take him to ride the barge today."

"We've got time," John said. "As much time as you need, Rachel."

* * *

Life with a child held so many lessons, Rachel thought. Lessons she might never have learned had Ben not come along. The C&O Canal experience provided her the awareness that it is sometimes the unplanned events that are remembered longer and more deeply than the careful orchestration that surrounds them.

Rachel and John paid for three tickets and waited in line for their turn to ride the barge, taking their seats on a boat filled with tourists wearing sweatshirts that advertised their visit to the nation's Capitol. Cameras flashed. Children laughed when one of the horses relieved itself mid-stride.

But the event Ben talked about most during supper after was not the outing they'd planned so carefully and paid for so dearly, but a chance encounter with an accordion player and his monkey dressed like a clown.

The musician stood on a street corner in Georgetown, the monkey holding a tin cup to collect money from passersby. Ben couldn't stop talking about it.

"Where do they live?" he wanted to know. When Rachel and John didn't know the answer, Ben became concerned they might be homeless and suggested Rachel invite the two to live with them.

"You let Mary and Belle come live with us when they didn't have a home," he reasoned.

"You just want to have the monkey around," John laughed.

"What do you think Ralph would do with a monkey in a clown suit in his house?"

Ben chewed on that through several bites of pizza, jumping next to thoughts of learning to play the accordion, thoughts of other money-making schemes, questions about monkeys as pets and whether the man had a wife at home.

Not a word about the C&O Canal ride. The most memorable part of the day was dressed in a clown suit and changed their whole focus. Sort of like my life, Rachel thought. The last thing I thought would happen to me in my sixties was a marriage proposal that included a child in the deal.

"What's the scowl all about?" John asked, startling her from her thoughts.

"Didn't know I was scowling."

"Well, you were," John said. Ben had left the table to scout out the bathroom in the pizza parlor. Public restrooms fascinated him. His trips to the men's rooms all over the city had become a family joke. He was very proud that in a few short months he had found the courage to make the trips by himself.

"Want to tell me what's on your mind? Ben should be gone on his adventure long enough so you can get a start, at least." John reached across the table and took her hands in his. They were large hands with long, gracefully tapering fingers. They were always warm.

"Is it Susan and Jim? Are you still worrying about them?"

Rachel had called her friend before they left the house. There had been no answer. Neither car was in the driveway when she looked across the street.

"Yes, I can't get Jim's look out of my mind. Shock. And then a look like he'd been kicked where it hurts the most. I felt like I was watching a huge hole open up between them, and I couldn't figure out how to bridge it for them."

Then Rachel remembered the horse dream from the night before. Standing at the edge of the chasm and feeling the horse brace to leap across. The dream always ended before she knew whether he tried. And whether he made it across.

"Rachel, this has nothing to do with you. I know you love Susan. I know you care about Jim, but you can't do a thing about what's going on in their marriage. It's their marriage. They'll work it out."

Rachel had just opened her mouth to try to say something – she didn't know what – when Ben burst back into the booth.

"It's the best!" he shouted. "The best bathroom of all."

Rachel laughed with relief. "What makes it the best, Ben?"

"Come with me, Rachel. Let me show you." He pulled her hand away from John's, tugging her toward the men's room.

"Ben, Rachel can't go to the men's room. She's a girl, remember."

"I'm so sorry, Rachel," Ben said, looking at her with pity, as if being a female was keeping her from doing some of the most thrilling things in life, starting with the men's room at Rockola.

"Rachel, we'll continue this conversation later. Seems like there's more going on here than what you're telling me."

Rachel smiled at the man across from her, trying to reassure him, but some very deep part of her wondered if he might be right. She knew Ben's bathroom adventure had provided only a very brief delay. She'd have to face whatever had prompted the dream. More importantly, she'd have to talk to John.

* * *

When Rachel walked into her office the next morning, Georgia wore the look on her face her boss had come to recognize as serious. Translated, the lowered eyebrows and pursed lips meant, "You've had enough time. This is the moment of decision."

"I know. I know," Rachel said as she leafed through the pink telephone message slips.

"So, are you going to call her?"

"Yes, I'm going to call Carrie today. Right now."

"And what are you going to tell her?"

Rachel hesitated long enough for Georgia to rev up her motor just a notch. "Rachel, what did you decide? You're not calling her to stall for time, are you? You promised me you'd make a decision by today, and that you'd call Carrie and Horace and tell them."

Rachel tucked the message slips in her pocket. Georgia pulled them out and walked past Rachel and into her office where she laid them out neatly and in order of priority on her desk near the phone.

Rachel followed her into the room. Sometimes her secretary's bossiness wasn't as welcome as others. This was one of those times.

Georgia stood with her arms crossed across her chest, waiting silently. Rachel knew she wouldn't move until she got what she wanted.

"I'm going to tell her I can't take the case. I'll recommend Henry Poston. He'll do a fine job. Horace knows him, and he'll be okay with that."

Georgia continued to stare.

"What's wrong with that?"

"I've never known you to turn down somebody who needed your help. It's John, isn't it? You didn't want to have to ask John for help. Still got some reservations, don't you?"

If you only knew, Rachel thought. She had tossed and turned most of the night, wrestling with the images of Jim's hurt face and of the damage done to a forty-year marriage by Susan's distrust. Of all that had created that distrust.

Rachel doubted that she would be able to weather that kind of storm, and she knew she didn't want to plunge a child into the potential chaos. She didn't even realize she was crying until Georgia handed her a tissue.

"What in the world? Rachel, what's going on?" The phone rang, but Georgia ignored it.

"Go ahead, get it," Rachel said.

"I'll let it roll into the answering service. I want you to sit down here and talk to me." Georgia patted the empty chair beside hers. Rachel blew her nose.

"I don't think I can marry John. I think we're moving too fast. We're too old. I'm too old. Too set in my ways. Too . . ."

"Too scared," Georgia interrupted. "You've just got cold feet. Don't worry. Everybody gets them the weeks before the wedding. They go away, I promise."

Rachel wanted to tell Georgia how much the situation with Susan and Jim had shaken her to the core, but she didn't want to betray a confidence. Even though she and Georgia had always shared each other's darkest secrets, Rachel didn't feel she could share Susan's.

Georgia sat waiting. "Okay, first things first." She left the room and came back with a chocolate chip cookie and handed it to Rachel with a glass of water. "Now, let's deal with Carrie. You want me to write a letter for you to sign, with a copy to Horace? You don't look like you're in any shape to call anybody on the phone."

"You're not going to try to talk me out of my decision?"

"Not this one," Georgia said. The phone rang, and she walked to her own desk to answer it.

Rachel nibbled on the cookie and looked at the stack of notebooks she'd have to return to Carrie. She felt a sense of relief at the thought that they'd soon be gone. She wondered what John would say when she told him. No way Georgia could handle that one.

* * *

The letter to Carrie was short and to the point. Georgia was good at that. One paragraph, thanking the young woman for thinking of Springer & Associates as she planned her action, a sentence explaining that she would be better served by another firm and a suggestion as to which firm that might be.

Period.

Rachel smiled as she thought about how beautifully simple Georgia was able to make life. She would have struggled for hours and ended up with a two-page letter that had been written and re-written to death. What a gift Georgia Payne was in her life.

She signed the letter and gave it back to Georgia to mail.

"Ready to talk about the other decision now?" Georgia asked.

Rachel put her head in her hands. "And I thought choosing a wedding gown was a problem," she moaned.

"I've got an idea," Georgia said, sitting on the edge of the chair in front of Rachel's desk. "Why don't you go out to the farm for a few days. Get away. Get some fresh air. In fact, why don't you take Belle and Mary. You've been promising them you'd show them the farm."

Rachel glanced down at her calendar. It was booked solid for the next few weeks. Georgia had tried to fit as many clients in during the weeks before the wedding so the newlyweds could get away on a two-week honeymoon.

Rachel groaned.

Georgia grabbed the calendar out of her hands. "I can take care of all this. Do what's important. Take care of yourself. Go. Belle is out of school all this week. You can leave tomorrow and be gone for four whole days."

Rachel admitted that the thought of getting away from the city felt like the thing to do. Except that she hated to leave Susan. Then a thought hit her. Maybe she could convince Susan to go, too. A road trip.

Georgia watched as the wheels turned. She knew to be quiet as Rachel processed the idea. She prayed.

"Okay, I'll do it," Rachel finally said, and Georgia busied herself by canceling appointments.

Rachel punched in Susan's number first and was relieved when her friend answered the phone on the first ring. "You must have been sitting beside the phone, waiting for my call," Rachel said.

"Actually, I was waiting for Jim's call," Susan chirped like a sixteen-year-old. "We're having lunch, and he's going to call to let me know where to meet him."

Rachel rose from her desk and walked over to the window. She needed to see something familiar out on the street. Something to ground her in reality. She felt like she'd been spun into some alternate world where the devastating scene in Susan's kitchen had all been an illusion. The hot dog vendor, talking on his cellphone on the street corner, reassured her that she was in DC.

"You sure sound perky," Rachel said.

"I am perky. I'm better than perky. I'm feeling on top of the world. I'm feeling . . ."

"Okay, I get the picture. No more clichés. I was calling to rescue you. To take you away from your horrible home life for a few days. I'm heading to the farm and wondered if you'd like to go with me."

Rachel could hear clattering sounds on the other end of the phone.

"Susan, did you hear me? What in the world are you doing?"

"Loading the dishwasher. Rachel (clatter, clatter) you can't go to the farm. We've got to find your wedding dress. (clatter, clatter) And I don't need to be rescued. I've never been happier in my life. Things are fine here. Rachel? Rachel, are you there?"

Rachel let out a long sigh. She felt relieved to hear that Susan's crisis had been resolved so quickly and wondered how many other times her marriage to Jim had teetered on the brink.

One thing she didn't wonder about and that was her own ability to go through such drama. Not enough meditation hours in a day to get me through something like that, she thought.

"Susan, I'm leaving for the farm in the morning. If you change your mind, be ready to leave by eight o'clock."

"But what about the dress? When are we …"

"There's not going to be a dress, Susan." Rachel said good-bye and hung up. A sense of relief fell over her like a warm baby blanket.

Chapter Nine

B elle sounded like a child who'd just been promised a trip to Disneyland when Rachel invited her to make the trip to Virginia. She said she could be packed in a matter of minutes.

"And I'll need to call Ricky and let him know we'll be gone."

"Oh," Rachel said. "I didn't know you'd decided to see him again." Belle hadn't mentioned Ricky's name since their conversation after he'd first made contact.

"Yes, we've been talking some," Belle said. "Every day, actually. He's doing really well, Rachel. Really well."

Right, Rachel thought. Another gullible woman. Another couple whose doomed relationship should be a warning to herself.

"Okay, Belle. You're a grown woman. Call Ricky. But I don't want him at the farm. This is a girls' getaway."

"A getaway? Why do YOU need to get away, Rachel? Shouldn't you be planning your wedding?"

"Be ready at eight, Belle. And don't ask too many questions. I don't have the answers."

* * *

Rachel's cousin Nancy apologized when Rachel called to ask about spending some time at the farm. Something rare had happened. Rare for a farmer. Nancy and Simon were going away for a week. George, the farm manager, would be left in charge. He'd let Rachel in the house and would be around to help should something go wrong. With an old house, that was always a possibility.

Rachel assured Nancy that they'd be fine. She'd miss her cousins but was delighted to hear that they were doing something she had encouraged them to do for years.

Rachel added another marriage to her list of ones she knew she couldn't survive.

"How are the wedding plans coming along?" Nancy asked before she hung up. Rachel pretended she hadn't heard, said "good-bye" and hung up the phone.

She waited until after dinner and Ben was in bed before she told John of her plans to be gone for the next four days. At first, he didn't say anything. He sat on the sofa beside her, staring straight ahead, struggling with the words that would express the fear sitting as solid as a stone under his ribcage.

John's heart beat hard under that weight, but it couldn't seem to move it. The weight lay heavy. He decided to say nothing except to question her plans for Ralph.

"I think I'll take him with me," Rachel said. "He loves the farm."

"What about Ben? They've grown inseparable."

When Rachel didn't respond, John saw the look she had tried to hide from him. He saw the fear. He sat with it for long enough to feel her fear loom larger than his own. When he had reached that place, he took her into his arms.

"We'll miss you, Rachel. But go, if this is what you need. And take Ralph. Looks like you may need him more than we will."

And then Rachel's tears fell and the hardness in John's chest melted as he held her to his heart.

* * *

As Rachel loaded her bag into the back of her black Volvo station wagon, Belle and Mary emerged from their basement apartment. When Ralph ran over to lick the child on her face, she squealed with delight.

"Ralph's going with us?" Belle asked. "What in the world will Ben do without his best friend?"

Rachel's glare stopped that line of questioning.

"Sorry," the young woman said. "Come on, Mary, hop in. Ralph can sit in the back with you."

She strapped the still sleepy little girl in her car seat and patted the empty space beside her. The dog jumped in and curled up with his head on Mary's lap. Just as Rachel started to pull out of the driveway, John ran out the front door, carrying a Tupperware container.

"Thought you might enjoy these leftover brownies on your trip," he said, leaning in the front window to give Rachel one last kiss goodbye.

"You're a lucky woman," Belle said as they drove off. Rachel looked into the rear view mirror and saw John still waving at her as they pulled onto Dupont Circle.

Rachel turned on the radio, a signal she hoped Belle would understand to mean she didn't want to talk. It worked. Belle pulled out a textbook and began to read. Mary and Ralph slept in the backseat. As soon as she left the city traffic, Rachel opened the Tupperware container and took out a brownie. On top lay a note that she left to read later.

Yes, I'm a lucky woman, she thought. And then monkey mind took over with images of how lucky she had imagined Susan was and how that luck had changed. I never did enjoy roller coasters, she reminded herself. Too much up and down. And I'm much too old to start riding them now.

She reached in for a second brownie. Belle looked over at her but didn't say a word.

"Want one?" Rachel asked.

"It's a little early for chocolate for me, but you go ahead."

"How's school?"

"Great. Got a test coming up next week after we go back. This time at the farm will be a great opportunity to catch up on some reading."

"I hope you'll give yourself a chance to enjoy the farm, too," Rachel said. "Get out in the fields and walk. Explore the woods. You and Mary may decide you want to trade the city life for the country."

Belle looked doubtful but promised she wouldn't spend every minute reading. She did devote the two hours in the car to the book, however, stopping only when Mary woke up and asked for a drink.

"Ralph drink," Mary said, offering the dog her sippy cup. Belle grabbed it just as the dog was about to give it a slobbery lick.

"Ralph will wait until we get to the farm, honey," Rachel said. "He likes to drink from the creek there."

Rachel pointed out a sign that indicated they only had five more miles to drive. She turned off the radio, which wasn't getting much more than static, and they rode the rest of the way in silence, interrupted only by the turning of pages and Mary's slurping.

Rachel looked in the rear view mirror and saw Ralph's big brown eyes staring at her. When the car turned down the long drive leading up to the farmhouse, the dog stood up on the seat. He knew where he was and wiggled with anticipation. Several cows stood at the fence as a welcoming committee, and, when Rachel stopped the car and opened the back door, Ralph ran over and leaped up on the railings to greet them.

"Cow," Mary crowed.

When Rachel looked surprised that a city child knew the word, Belle laughed. "We practiced last night after you called. She can also say 'horse' and 'barn,' too."

"That about covers it," Rachel laughed.

George walked around the side of the house, arms outstretched.

Assuming the welcome was for her, Mary ran to him. He laughed and picked her up. "Obviously, nobody's taught her about strangers," he said, walking toward the two women.

"We're working on it," Belle said, holding out her hand.

"George, this is Belle and her daughter Mary," Rachel said. George handed the child to her mother and wrapped Rachel in a bear hug. When they parted, he stepped back to get a good look at her. Their eyes locked in silence.

"It's good to see you again, Rachel," he said. "Very good."

Rachel smiled, picked up her bag and walked toward the house where she had spent so much of her childhood. The years when life was less complicated. Ralph bounded up the stairs behind her. When she opened the door, he was the first inside, always the protector, sniffing for danger. Satisfied that all was well, at least in the hall, he turned and looked back at his mistress as if to say, "It's okay. Come on in."

Rachel laughed. "Thanks, boy." She patted his head. "We're safe."

* * *

Rachel unpacked her small bag and surveyed the sunny guest room at the top of the stairs. Her cousin had placed a bud vase with a single yellow rose on the bedside table. She bent over to sniff, letting the scent filter through her body. She reached out and gently touched the delicate petals. John frequently brought her roses for no other reason that he loved her. Rachel shook her head, trying to stop the thoughts of what she had left behind.

I need to clear my head of him for a few days, she told herself. Need a fresh perspective. Obviously, the intention was good but perhaps impossible, since she had just arrived and already her thoughts were focused on John.

Rachel walked over to the window that looked out over the front lawn. There George played keep-away with Ralph while Mary squealed with delight nearby. Belle perched on the rope swing that hung from the ancient oak tree at the corner of the yard.

Rachel smiled and took a deep breath. George seemed to have gotten taller since the last time she saw him. Farm life obviously agreed with him, Rachel thought as she realized his posture had straightened, adding a couple of inches to his height. Pride in a job well done, she thought, admiring the fresh coat of paint on the fence that lined the long driveway.

As she watched him lope over to where Belle swung, she thought the limp appeared less pronounced, too. She wondered if the nightmares he had told her he suffered since his time in Vietnam had gone away.

Rachel left her room and passed by the open door to the larger guestroom at the other end of the hall. She smiled when she saw that Belle had unpacked Mary's favorite stuffed animals and perched them on one of the twin beds.

Feels like home, she thought, as she descended the stairs. George met her at the door. "How was the drive down?" he asked. "Much traffic?"

"Almost none," Rachel said.

"How about some coffee? I made a pot about an hour ago. Thought you might like a cup when you arrived."

"Very thoughtful of you, George. Think I will." Rachel poured the rich, black brew into one of her favorite mugs and settled into the rocking chair beside the kitchen wood stove.

"I'm not going to leave here until I see your photographs," she said.

"Well, then, I guess I'll have to keep you waiting for a long time, won't I?"

Rachel laughed. "We're staying four days. Belle has an exam on Monday, and I have clients waiting."

"And a wedding."

Rachel turned her head from George and looked around the kitchen, trying to find something which would change the focus.

"What's this?" George asked. "Do I sense some second thoughts here?"

"My, goodness, where do I have to go to get away from these questions? To get some privacy?" Rachel blurted out before she could stop herself. George's raised eyebrows and furrowed brow made her realize he'd been joking and that her reaction had caught him off guard.

"I'm sorry, George. How rude of me. Guess I'm feeling a little stressed about the whole thing."

"Guess you are. Maybe a walk would help. How about it? I've got something I've been wanting to show you down near the river."

"Sounds like the perfect idea. Let me go change my shoes."

George said he'd meet her at the barn in five minutes. As she walked up the stairs to her room, she glanced out the window and saw Ralph trailing George as he left the yard.

* * *

Belle and Mary met Rachel on the steps as she walked down a few minutes later. The little girl rubbed her eyes and sniffled. "We're going to lie down and take a little nap," Belle said. "Long drive and too much excitement."

Rachel said she's rustle up some lunch when she got back from her walk to the river with George. "Ralph's going with us. Will you be okay by yourself?" she asked.

"We're fine. Enjoy your walk."

When Rachel reached the bottom of the steps, she looked back at the two. Mary was already asleep in her mother's arms. What a lucky little girl to have a mother so focused on making you feel loved, she thought. She didn't think of her own mother often. After all, she'd been dead almost fifty years, and Rachel could hardly remember the days before she had fallen to her death from the back of a horse.

Many loving women, including her grandmother, had helped her father raise his two children in the years afterward. And in her adult life, women friends had continued to fill the role of mother for her. But sometimes, when she observed a special look pass between a young mother and her child, Rachel felt a longing.

She closed the front door quietly so as not to disturb the sleeping child and walked toward the barn. Ralph saw her coming and ran down the hill toward her. The farm always seemed to take at least five years off Ralph's life, and he leaped and bounded toward her like a puppy. At one point, he stopped to grab a stick in his mouth and rushed toward her to play fetch. Rachel pulled the stick out of his jaws and tossed it toward George, waiting at the barn.

"This dog is a natural born farm dog. You need to move him out of that dirty old city to a place where he can run free like he was meant to," George said.

"Do you hear that, Ralph? He wants to take you away from the pigeons and all your friends on the Circle. The whole Capitol would collapse if Ralph left town. He's one of the chief ambassadors there, aren't you, boy?"

Ralph ran between the two, back and forth. Finally, George threw the stick toward the woods. Ralph ran into the underbrush but couldn't find it.

"Come on, Ralph, we've got something to show your mistress." Ralph came when he was called and trotted off down the path through the woods in front of them.

"The farm looks wonderful, George. You've done miracles with the place."

George stared off into the woods and didn't say anything, but Rachel knew he was grateful for her compliment. "I'm happy here,

Rachel," he finally said. "I didn't think I'd ever be happy again. Didn't think I'd ever work again. Feel safe."

They walked on for a while in companionable silence, listening to the woods sounds. Ralph chased several squirrels, occasionally looking back to make sure Rachel had seen his bravery.

"My cousins are lucky to have found you. I'm afraid they were getting overwhelmed by the place and had started to let it get pretty run down."

"I love this farm, and they're good to share it with me. There's only one problem."

Rachel waited. She knew from her professional experience not to push. Finally, she stopped and turned to him. "What is it, George? Something I can do to help?"

"I get lonely, Rachel," he said. She could see his shoulders sag with the loneliness. "Your cousins have each other. They're still so much in love, and sometimes I feel like a fifth wheel. They don't mean to make me feel that way. In fact, they go out of their way to include me in everything they do, but . . ."

"I know, George," Rachel said, walking on toward the river. Even though she didn't. Rachel had that unusual ability to be totally fulfilled alone. She'd never really known what lonely felt like. All her life, friends had felt sorry for her being single, but she'd never wanted to change that status. Never felt the need. She was the exception, she knew. George was the rule.

Suddenly, he veered off the path toward the river and inched his way down the bank to the water. Ralph leaped over the edge toward him. George held up his hand to help Rachel down the incline.

It was only after she reached the sandy beach that she saw what he had wanted to show her. A tower of rocks stood like a monument in the middle of the water. At its highest, it was taller than George and about as wide as a refrigerator.

"It just appeared one day," George said. "I have no idea who did it or why, but he, or she, must have been tall."

"And strong," Rachel said. "Some of these rocks are heavy." She reached out to touch the artwork. The sun created a mosaic of colors that glistened with the water. "It's beautiful," she whispered. "What a beautiful surprise. Thank you for sharing it with me. Thank you."

Ralph lay in the water looking up at the rocks and the people admiring them. And then, without warning, he leaped to attention and rushed around and around it, splashing water in a mad dance of utter glee.

"This dog is crazy," George laughed.

"No, just happy," Rachel said.

"Me, too," George said and joined Ralph in his water celebration. He grabbed Rachel's hand, and the three splashed around the river rocks until Rachel became dizzy and begged to stop.

"We wore her out, Ralph," George said, joining Rachel where she sat on the riverbank. Ralph came to sit next to the two where they rested, admiring the mysterious tower.

"Have you shown this to my cousins?" Rachel asked. "Maybe they'd have some idea who did it."

"I haven't shared it with anyone except you. Didn't want to. In fact, I don't think I want to know who did it. Might spoil the magic. You do believe in magic, don't you, Rachel?"

Rachel started to laugh and then realized that George was serious. She didn't know exactly what to say.

"What, did they make you swear you didn't believe in magic when you took the bar exam?" he teased her.

"Yeah, I think one of the courses my first year of law school covered all the reasons why magic couldn't possibly hold up in court."

George shook his head and reached out and patted her hand. "Stuck in the city and doesn't believe in magic. Not sure there's any hope for you, lady. Unless . . ."

"Unless what?"

"Unless you'll race me back to the barn," George yelled and clamored up the rise and headed toward the path. He turned back. "If you can't beat a one-legged old guy, you're hopeless. If you can, we'll talk about the next step." And off he loped, Ralph behind him.

Rachel had lost her breath by the time she reached the barn. She looked back and saw that Ralph had stayed by George's side, sensing he needed a friend in the race he soundly lost.

"What in the world are you two doing?" Belle yelled from the back porch. "Rachel, are you okay? What's wrong?"

Rachel caught her breath for a few minutes. George limped over and stuck out his hand to shake hers.

"Nothing's wrong," she yelled. "We were running a race, that's all."

"And she won," George panted. "There's hope. After dinner, we'll take the next step in our efforts to retrieve your magic. In the meantime, don't get too cocky. I only have one leg, remember."

Belle and Mary walked over to where the two stood laughing together. Belle shook her head, totally baffled by the scene before her. "I don't know what's going on here, Mary, but it looks like whatever it is, they're having fun.

Chapter Ten

R achel wondered about the next step that would cure her disbelief in magic. As soon as the supper dishes had been washed, dried and put away, she approached George.

"Okay, let's have it," she said.

"Have what?" he asked, feigning innocence. "Not even a 'thank you, George, for the wonderful vegetable soup you brought down so we wouldn't starve?' No 'thanks, George, for letting us eat your last three pieces of apple pie so we wouldn't suffer a no-dessert meal?'"

"John brownies," Mary chirped from the antique highchair in which she sat to survey the kitchen clean-up. Rachel saw a shadow pass over George's face.

"Smart little girl," he said. "How old is she now? Three going on 23? Not much gets by her."

"I'll say," Rachel replied. "But I do thank you for the soup and the excellent pie. I'll go into town tomorrow and load up on groceries so you won't have to feed us again."

"It was my pleasure, madam," George said with a regal bow. "My pleasure, indeed. And now, if you'll come with me, we'll take the next step in your recovery program."

Rachel lifted Mary out of the highchair and switched off the kitchen light. "Where are we going?" she asked.

"Where we go?" Mary echoed.

"You're staying here with your mother," George said, taking the child from Rachel's arms and carrying her into the sitting room where Belle sat, studying.

Mary began to whine, "Me go. Me go." Ralph licked her hand.

"No, you stay here, baby," her mother said. "Heaven knows what these two are up to, and it's your bedtime."

George pulled Rachel out of the room before Mary could start up another chorus of "Me, too."

"Where are we going?" Rachel asked.

"My place. Right across the field. It's time for you to see my real work. My heart work. The place where magic is made."

Rachel looked up at the heavens as she stepped off the front porch. Stars speckled the sky like sparkling confetti stuck in a net above them, ready to fall at the yank of some invisible cord. She smiled.

"What's the smile coming from?" George asked.

Rachel walked on for a few minutes in silence, wondering if she should admit how much she loved country nights. Their running debate over the benefits of city life over country life had gone on since they met. Rachel, being a debater by profession, wasn't sure she was ready to concede even an inch to George.

Finally, she spoke. "The stars are so bright. Like the lights of Broadway."

"Hrumph," George said. "Broadway can't touch these lights. They never go out. Even on a cloudy night, they're up there shining through. Knowing they're up there is what's gotten me through some of my nights."

Rachel resisted her temptation to continue the debate and walked on in silence. She felt something she didn't allow herself to feel very often. She felt the desire to admit George was right. To agree with him. She felt it but stopped short of agreeing out loud. She wasn't ready to go that far.

As they drew near the farm manager's house at the edge of the pond, they stopped to look at the moon, nearly full and reflected in the water. A bullfrog croaked, the sound echoing through the night.

The wings of a flock of chimney swallows rustled overhead.

Rachel inhaled a deep breath. George took her hand and led her toward the house. Rachel felt the calluses and realized how much they felt like her father's work-worn hands. George squeezed her fingers.

"Welcome, Rachel Springer, to my humble abode."

The front door opened into a long hall with two sitting rooms on either side. A tall grandfather clock chimed the hour as the two stood at the entrance.

"Here, let me take your coat," George said, lifting it from her shoulders and hanging it on the coat tree beside the door. It looked at home there beside a leather bomber's jacket and a yellow slicker. "Come on in here while I light a fire," he said, indicating a rocking chair. Rachel sat, and he covered her legs with a crocheted afghan.

"This looks familiar," she said. "I believe my grandmother made it."

"I believe you're right. The house is filled with her work. Afghans, bedspreads, doilies, placemats. Sometimes I feel a little overwhelmed by the laciness of it all."

"I don't think you need to worry about your masculinity, George. It seems firmly intact, to me."

"Wait until you see me build a fire, lady." George knelt down on the hearth and within minutes, a fire roared.

"Can I get you something to drink? A little wine perhaps?"

"Sure, that sounds nice."

George disappeared into the kitchen, leaving Rachel to look around at the changes in the room since she had last visited the house where her father had spent his childhood. Her grandparents had built the larger house up the hill when their family had outgrown the two bedrooms here. The feel of family remained even though George lived alone.

The marks where her grandparents had measured her father's

growth were still on the front door sill and her grandmother's porcelain dolls on the mantel beneath her wedding portrait. But several masculine touches were tucked here and there where George had claimed his turf. An ashtray and a can of Prince Albert's tobacco. The pipe lay cold on the top of the tin.

Cowboy boots stood beside the fireplace where they had been polished. Rachel caught a whiff of the polish and inhaled deeply. That smell reminds me of my father, too, she thought. And then she realized that being at the farm brought back so many memories of the country man that she almost found herself forgetting her love of the city.

George walked into the room, carrying two wine glasses and a bottle under his arm. He sat in the rocking chair facing hers and set the bottle on a small table beside him. Handing her a glass, he said, "Hope you like burgundy. It's all I have."

"Burgundy is good. Just don't let me drink more than one glass. Red wine gives me a headache if I drink too much."

"You're safe with me, lady."

The two sat quietly, listening to the tick of the hall clock and the crackle of the fire. A dim lamp in a far corner provided the only light to compete with the stars outside.

"You seem to be at home here," Rachel finally said.

"I never thought it would happen. Never thought I'd ever have another home. Didn't even want to live, much less live happily."

"How did you meet my cousins?"

"Simple. I answered their ad for a farm manager."

"Had you ever been a farm manager before?"

"No, but it's not rocket science. Where there's a will, there's a way. I was desperate for peace and quiet. And some space. And escape from people. All the things you love about the city, I wanted to get away from. And your cousins gave me a chance. A crash course in milking cows, feeding the animals, mending fences. Along the way, I've learned to be a midwife, to shoe horses and trap varmints. And as a reward, I've gotten the peace I was looking for in this place that's become my home." George swept his arms around the room to include the porcelain dolls. "The dead – your dead – have become my family. It's been like magic. Speaking of which, are you ready for your next step into the realm of magic?" George took another sip of wine and set his glass down.

Rachel felt her face flush and gulped at her drink. She was afraid that the magic might involve some kind of romantic overture she wasn't sure she knew how to handle. She was engaged to be married in two weeks and yet her feelings for the man sitting across from her were warm. Too warm for a soon-to-be married woman.

But Rachel was not the kind of woman to walk away from a challenge. She stood and wrapped the afghan around her shoulders like a shield. "Sure, show me your magic."

"Follow me," George said and walked across the hall to the other sitting room. He waited until she had reached his side and then flicked on the overhead light.

Rachel gasped and grabbed the door frame to steady herself. Faces. Three walls covered with 4 x 6 photographs of faces. Black and white with white borders, frameless. Eyes stared straight at the camera. All dark eyes, dark hair. All children. At first glance, they looked like the same Vietnamese child, but a subtle difference could be discerned in each of the hundreds of shots.

Speechless, Rachel walked around the room, studying each child, each pair of hungry eyes. One little girl sucked her thumb in the universal symbol of security. A baby suckled a bare breast. A teenager carried a rifle.

Tears streaming down her face, Rachel turned to George and let out a deep sigh. "You took all these?"

George nodded. "They kept me alive. Kept me sane. Taking the pictures. Preserving these children. Some of them probably didn't make it through the war." He reached out and touched the image of the boy with the rifle. Each picture had a name written in black ink in the bottom border. "Kim" was the boy with the gun.

"Come," George said and led her up the stairs to another room, also turned into a gallery. These walls were similarly papered, this time with cows. The same brown eyes. Names on the pictures.

Rachel laughed with relief.

"More magic," George said. "These kept me alive, too. Kept me sane. Connected me as I tried to find my place in my own country. The place I'd lost. It's been my magic. The camera has been my lens into another world. A world beyond my own suffering. Some of these didn't make it either," George said, pointing to one gentle face. "Grace died giving birth to a calf last spring." He gently touched the image and moved on to another photograph. "But they're all still here," he said, placing his hand on his chest. "It's magic what a difference connecting with another soul can make to a broken man."

Rachel nodded. Just as she was about to speak, she was interrupted by a barking downstairs at the front door. George laughed. "Sounds like Ralph wants to join the magic. Shall I let him in?"

"Please," Rachel said.

"He doesn't let you get too far out of his sight, does he?"

"No. I think he'd agree with you about magic and the connections we make with others."

Ralph bounded through the front door, sniffed at George and ran over to stand protectively beside Rachel.

"Smart dog," George said.

"Very," Rachel agreed and rubbed Ralph behind one ear.

"Walk you back down the hill?"

"Well, looks like I've got an escort, thank you. We'll be fine." Rachel hung the afghan on the banister and shrugged into her coat. She kissed George on the cheek and opened the door to leave.

"Thanks for sharing this with me, George. It's powerful."

"Thank you, Rachel. I knew you'd get it. Not everybody does, you know, and I'm careful who I show it to. Magic can be spoiled if you're not careful. I don't want anybody to try to talk me out of believing. That would be the end of me, I'm sure. Not believing in magic.

* * *

When Rachel walked in the house, she felt its silence drop around her like a cloak. Ralph ran upstairs to check on Belle and Mary. Rachel heard giggles and knew the bedtime ritual continued in full swing. She walked into the kitchen and saw the message light on the answering machine blink.

"Hey, Rachel. It's me," John's voice said. "Tried your cellphone but your inbox is full, and I couldn't leave a message. Call me. I love you. We miss you." Ben's voice chimed in with, "I love you, too. I miss you gobs. When's she coming home, Granddad?" The machine clicked off before John had time to answer the child. Rachel wondered what the answer had been. She hadn't been clear about a return date when she left.

Rachel erased the message and walked out to the back porch to return the call so that her voice wouldn't interfere with the bedtime preparations.

John answered on the first ring.

"You must have been sitting right by the phone. How are you?"

"We're fine. How are things at the farm? Not planning to abandon us for Farmboy, are you?"

Rachel laughed nervously. One of the things she loved about John was his directness. He had a fresh way of cutting right to the chase rather than stuffing his feelings. Sometimes the childlike way he communicated still shocked Rachel. This was one of those times.

"Things here are fine," she said. "Mary and Belle are really enjoying themselves. They helped George with the milking this afternoon."

"How about you? Did you help George with the milking?"

"No, John. I've done my share of milking in the past. It just doesn't appeal to me anymore."

"Good."

A moment of silence and then John launched into the neighborhood news. The Mosers had started work on a new deck. Susan and Jim called to say they'd be gone for a few days to Alabama to visit their son and his family.

"Wow. I can't believe Jim actually took some time off. He's been working so hard lately."

"Yeah. Susan sounded like a newlywed. She was really excited. Said to tell you 'thanks' and that she was sorry to skip out on the wedding dress mission."

More silence.

"Yeah, well, I'll give her a call and reassure her that all is well."

"Is all well, Rachel?"

"All is well, John. Give Ben a kiss goodnight for me. And save one for yourself."

"Love you."

"Love you, too, John. We'll talk tomorrow." Rachel hung up. She still felt the magic of the photos and didn't want conversations about decks and other trivia to dilute the experience.

She walked back inside and then upstairs to draw a bath. As the tub filled, Rachel slowly undressed. Her body still ached from the drive and sleeping in a strange bed. She poured some Epsom salts in the hot water and eased her body down into its warmth.

Now, *THIS* is magic, she thought and closed her eyes, breathing in the moist air. Breathing in. Breathing.

It was so easy to say "all is well." And she knew it was good to speak positive thoughts and that her brain needed to hear her say the words. But believing it on a cellular level was another matter. Rachel knew her body well enough to know that deep down, she didn't believe that all was well. Down deep, she was a scared little girl. Afraid that she was about to make a serious mistake that would hurt not just her, but John and Ben. Especially Ben.

She looked down at the Scooby Doo "marriage ring" that Ben had insisted she wear on the trip. Rachel smiled at the memory of the night when the child had loaned the ring to his grandfather with the suggestion that he give it to Rachel so they could get married and sleep together like his parents.

Oh, if it were that simple, Rachel thought as she sank deeper into the warm bath water.

Chapter Eleven

A timid knock on her bedroom door woke Rachel the next morning. When she opened her eyes, she saw that the sun had risen over the top of the row of maple trees that lined the driveway. She looked at the clock on her bedside table and then looked again to verify the time. Ten o'clock. She couldn't remember the last time she had slept that late.

"Rachel, are you alive in there?" Belle asked, cracking the door and peeping into the room.

Rachel rubbed her eyes and swung her legs out of the nest of covers. "I can't believe I slept this late," she said. "Thanks for checking on me."

"Well, I wasn't sure if I should wake you or not, but it's so unlike you to sleep late, I got worried."

Rachel slid her feet into slippers and wrapped the old flannel robe around herself. "Yeah, this place has a way of relaxing me, I guess."

"It's like magic."

Rachel's head jerked up. How did Belle know? Had she been spying on them last night? Of course not, silly, Rachel thought. It's a saying lots of people use. "It's magic."

"How about some coffee?" Belle asked. "I just made a fresh pot."

"Thanks," Rachel said and padded down the stairs behind Belle. Mary sat on the kitchen floor, coloring book and crayons spread out on the hook rug near the fireplace. She looked up at Rachel and beamed, proudly holding up a brightly colored page and crowing with ecstasy.

Leigh Somerville

"Mary loves it here," Belle said. "Thank you so much for bringing us."

Rachel nodded and sat down at the kitchen table where she had eaten so many meals in the past. The large kitchen held many memories, and Rachel let herself sink into the slow pace of country life. A cow lowed somewhere in the distance, and the sound drifted toward her like music, like a lullaby to Rachel's ears.

"George called a little while ago to ask if Mary and I would like to drive to town with him to buy some feed for the animals. I didn't want to leave without telling you where we're going," Belle said. "He said he thought Mary would enjoy the feed store. Said they might have some baby chickens for her to pet."

Rachel surprised herself with a feeling she couldn't immediately identify. Jealousy? That old familiar feeling of being left out? She jerked her emotions back into control.

"Sounds like a good idea."

"You'll be okay here by yourself, won't you?"

"Sure," Rachel said. "Think I'll spend some time in the attic. During my last visit, Nancy said there were some boxes up there with my name on them. Think I'll check them out and see what can be gotten rid of and what needs to go back to the city with me."

Mary's delighted squeals announced George's arrival even before his knock on the backdoor. The child ran to open it and leaped into his arms. His eyes found Rachel's over the top of the girl's head. "Sleep well?" he asked.

"Like magic," Rachel said. "Sounds like you guys have a fun adventure planned."

"Need anything in town? I'll be glad to pick up stuff for you if you want to give me a list."

"No, I think we're well supplied. After all, we're not staying long."

George looked at her and the light disappeared from his eyes. "I know," he said.

Mary tightened her grip on his leg. "Me go. Me go." Belle laughed. "I sure hope you won't be sorry you took us with you. She's very excited."

"I won't be sorry. I'm glad for the company of two beautiful females. Come on, let's get Mary's car seat and put it in my truck. Never had this experience before. Should be quite an adventure."

More magic, Rachel thought, and then felt the pang again as the three walked out of the kitchen, leaving her alone in the empty room.

* * *

Rachel decided to wait until after she'd finished exploring the attic before she took a shower. She knew she'd be covered by dust in no time at all.

When she pulled the cord that dangled from the bare overhead bulb hanging just inside the door to the large room, memories of afternoons spent playing dress-up flooded over her. She walked to the large camelback trunk she remembered as her favorite treasure chest of old clothes.

When she lifted the lid, the same mounds of mothball smelling dresses lay right where she'd left them. She smiled as she lifted a red calico apron and shook it out. It looked so much smaller than it had years ago when she had used it to play waitress with her friend Robert.

She remembered the little boy seated at a door stretched across a pair of sawhorses, pretending that it was a cafe counter where she served him mud pies. Where is Robert now, she wondered. Does he remember this attic?

Rachel closed the trunk lid and searched for the boxes her cousin had said were labeled with her name. After crawling around on her hands and knees in three of the far corners, she found them neatly stacked near the entrance to the attic.

Too easy, she laughed. Why do I always try the hardest paths first?

The first box contained the manger scene Rachel remembered arranging on the top of the upright piano every Christmas. Inside the box was a note which read "To whom it may concern: If you're wondering why there are only two Wise Men, a little black puppy named Sam ate the third."

Rachel laughed. Sam had settled into the slow pace of an old dog by the time she met him, but she had grown up hearing lots of Sam stories. She tucked the note back in the box and patted the lid shut with a chuckle. "You were a good friend, Sam, wherever you are now."

The second box was full of handmade decorations for every possible holiday on the calendar. Tiny cotton ball Easter bunnies. Turkeys made from clothespins. Pumpkins cut out of orange construction paper. And candy canes still sticky in cellophane. Rachel's grandmother had been a decorator and every inch of the old farmhouse was her palate.

Ben will love all this stuff, Rachel thought as she shoved the boxes closer to the door.

On the lid of the third large, flat box, "Garfinkle's," the name of a large department store, was embossed in gold letters. When Rachel untied the blue ribbon and lifted the lid, she found layers and layers of limp tissue paper. Slowly, carefully, she peeled them back. She didn't realize she'd been holding her breath until she let it out in a loud gasp at the sight of a wedding dress. An envelope lay on top of the ivory bodice. No name was written on it and it had not been sealed. With no effort, Rachel withdrew her grandmother's monogrammed notecard and opened it to find one sentence.

"To whomever wears this dress after me, may you find the magic I found in love."

Rachel carried the box down the stairs and into the front parlor where she could remove the folds of filmy organza in the morning sunlight that streamed in the front windows.

The bodice was stitched in tucks that folded into an empire waist of heavy brocade. The organza skirt fell to the floor like clouds, creating an angelic effect that did, indeed, look like magic.

Rachel held the dress up in front of her pajamas and walked over to the giant mirror that hung over the mantle. She stared at her reflection. She didn't even need to try it on to know that it would fit perfectly. She didn't even need to get a second opinion. Not even Susan's. She knew her grandmother's dress was what she'd wear on her own wedding day.

* * *

"Susan, I found my dress."

"Hello? Who is this?"

"What do you mean 'WHO IS THIS?' It's me. Rachel."

"Rachel? Where are you?"

"I'm at the farm with Belle and Mary. We came down for a few days to get away. It's beautiful here. So relaxing. Just what I needed."

"Good grief, Rachel. How can you be relaxed at a time like this? There are things to be done, and we've got less than two weeks before the wedding. You don't even have a dress."

Rachel rose from the stool where she sat holding the wall phone away from her ear while Susan jabbered on and on. Finally, when the jabbering stopped, she cradled the receiver against her neck again.

"Susan, you didn't hear me. I found a dress."

At first, all Rachel heard was silence at the other end of the line. Then, Susan's voice screeched, "Without me? You bought a dress without me?"

"I didn't say I BOUGHT a dress. I said I FOUND a dress. In the attic here. It was my grandmother's. It's perfect."

"And it fits? And it's not moldy or yellow or something else awful like that?"

"No, Susan. It's not any of those things."

"Well, I don't know, Rachel."

"I'll be back day after tomorrow. You can see for yourself." Rachel knew that somehow she'd have to let Susan believe she'd played a part in finding the dress, but she wasn't sure how. Time for figuring that out later. "How are things across the street? Seen my boys lately?"

"Ben looks mighty sad without Ralph. And John . . . Well, I wouldn't leave that man alone too much, Rachel. You know how men are."

Rachel laughed at Susan's warning and then stopped herself from joking about a matter that had so recently shaken her best friend to her very core. Even though Susan had no real basis for thinking her husband had been unfaithful, the tricks her mind played had left scars. Rachel knew to be gentle.

"I'll be home soon. You'll love the dress."

"We'll see. We've still got to decide on flowers, you know. And Stan called yesterday and said Lily's been coughing, and they're not sure whether she's got the swine flu. And . . ."

"Okay. Okay. Susan, I'm starting to get nervous again. Let up on me, will you. I'll be afraid to come home."

"Okay, but . . ."

"Bye, Susan."

Just as Rachel hung up the phone, she heard George's truck pull into the backyard. Doors slammed, and Ralph greeted everybody with several loud barks. When Rachel looked out the window over the kitchen sink, she saw the dog run in circles around George. Mary rode on his shoulders. Belle laughed up at her daughter, pried her little hands off George's eyes and the three moved toward the house in a tumble of barking and laughter.

Rachel folded the wedding dress back into its bed of tissue paper, tucking the note inside.

"What you got there?" Belle asked, peering over Rachel's shoulder just as she was about to retie the ribbons.

"It's my grandmother's wedding dress. Found it in the attic in one of those boxes Nancy told me about. I'm going to take it home, have it cleaned and wear it." Rachel lifted the lid so Belle could catch a glimpse.

"Rachel, it's lovely. Will it fit you?"

"I think so, Belle. I think it's the one." The door closed gently on the other side of the room, and she turned to see George heading back out to his truck.

"Where's he going?" Belle asked. "I thought he was going to come in and have lunch with us. Men. You just never know."

"He'll be back, honey. Maybe he went to get something."

"Maybe."

"Looks like you all had fun. See any baby chickens?"

Belle scooped Mary up in her arms and spun the tale of the morning's adventure at the feed store. No baby chickens but some rabbits had tickled Mary's fancy.

"George was amazing with her. So gentle and patient." Belle looked at Rachel and blushed, tucking a loose strand of hair behind her ear.

"Why, Belle, I believe you've got a crush on the man."

"Women my age don't get crushes. I do like him, though."

"Me too! Me too!" Mary chimed. "Me like George."

"What about Ricky?" Rachel asked.

Belle looked out the window, her eyes following the rusted red truck down the lane. "Yeah, what about Ricky." The young woman turned back to face Rachel. "Ricky and I met when we were both drunks, Rachel. I'm changing. He's changing."

Rachel nodded. She finished tying the ribbon around the box and tucked it under her arm. "You'll figure it out, Belle. We usually do."

* * *

Later that afternoon, the phone rang, interrupting Rachel's nap. She ran into the hall and grabbed the phone on its last ring before the call rolled into the answering machine.

Rachel's heart skipped a beat when she heard her secretary's voice. She knew Georgia wouldn't call except to report bad news.

"What is it, Georgia?"

"Horace had a heart attack this morning," Georgia said. Rachel knew without hearing the words that the story didn't have a happy ending. Georgia was subdued. "The funeral is Friday at eleven o'clock."

Rachel slid down to the floor with her back against the wall. She listened to the silence. The grandfather clock at the bottom of the stairs ticked away the minutes. Rachel felt tears rise to the surface and knew she needed to take care of business before she let them surface.

"Go on home, Georgia. Close the office and take the rest of the day off." When Georgia started to object, Rachel cut her off. "Georgia, I'm your boss, remember. Go home. I'll be back tomorrow, and we'll see what needs to be done."

"I guess I could bake some cookies," Georgia muttered.

"Yes, go bake cookies. That's important. Horace loved your cookies."

At those words, Georgia began to sniffle. After several seconds of trying to control her tears, she hung up. Rachel sat cradling the phone, listening to the dial tone. Finally, she laid the receiver in the cradle and stood up.

"Who was that?" Belle asked, coming out of the bathroom down the hall. "You don't look so good."

"Georgia. Horace Gilbert died this morning. Heart attack."

Belle patted Rachel on the back. In some way, the young woman was wise beyond her years. She knew that sometimes there were no words as comforting as a gentle touch.

"Think I'll take Ralph and go for a walk," Rachel said. "We'll be back before supper."

Belle nodded. "I'll cook," she said.

Rachel smiled. "That's what Georgia's doing. Fixing food. Funny. That's what women do, isn't it? When the world is falling apart, we head for the kitchen." Rachel started down the stairs, Ralph close at her heels. Most women, she thought, but some of us go for a walk with our dogs.

Ralph seemed to sense Rachel's mood and matched his pace to it. Instead of bounding off the porch and leaping at the squirrels at the edge of the woods, he slowly picked his way down the steps, staying close beside his mistress.

"Which way, boy? Which way to go?"

Ralph looked first toward the highway, seeming to study its possibilities, then toward the barn, quickly nixing that choice and turning to face the woods. He tugged at Rachel's jacket and set off ahead of her at a quick trot. Rachel followed.

The quiet of the woods created a world of its own. The tall evergreens formed a canopy overhead, blocking out the bright afternoon sun. The dim light felt safe. The breeze that stirred the leaves in the yard was absent within the woods and Rachel felt like she had stepped into a protective vacuum.

This is where Horace is now, she thought. Away from all the frantic activity of his life. She thought about the wall of file cabinets she had accumulated over the years of representing Horace and all his schemes. All gone. No more scrapping to get to the top of the heap. No more clawing at those who tried to get the better of him. All gone now.

Rachel had never talked to Horace about death, except to encourage him to write a will. She didn't know if he believed in life after death. She didn't know for sure that she did. Still, if there were something for Horace to go to, she hoped he felt the same relief there that she felt in the quiet of the woods.

She heard a splash and realized that Ralph had jumped in the creek and was heading her way with a stick in his mouth. So much for quiet, she laughed. She threw the stick a couple of times and then sat on a tree stump. A perfect place to meditate, she thought. Ralph knew the routine and lay down quietly next to her. He dropped the stick beside him and rested his head on his paws. Within a few minutes, his snoring was added to the woods sounds. A small animal rustled in the leaves behind Rachel. A squirrel scurried up a tree, setting off the squawking of a bird perched on a branch overhead. The tiny waterfall George had shown her the night before provided a steady background noise as Rachel focused on her breath.

She breathed in the spirit of the woods. She breathed out the phone call and the sound of Georgia's grief. She breathed in the decaying of the leaves, the flowing of the water, the passing of the life around her. She breathed out the memories of Horace in his bodily form. The weak heart. The cigarettes. The martinis. The angry red face she had seen across her desk all those years. Breathing. Breathing. Breathing until Rachel's mind floated free of Horace into the woods around her and became one with the non-thinking place where there is no suffering. Only a dog snoring beside a waterfall.

Chapter Twelve

S orry to hear about your friend," George said to Rachel as she
approached the barn.

"Wow, news travels fast, even here on the farm," she
laughed. George smiled and opened his arms to offer a hug. Rachel
walked into his embrace with a relief that was still new to her.

"When I went up to the house to get Mary for the milking, Belle
told me," George said, stroking Rachel's hair. She lifted her head
from his chest and looked at the ruddy cheeks and the deep crows
feet around his dark eyes.

"Sounds like you're trying to make farm girls out of my
downstairs neighbors, George. Good thing I'm taking them back to
the city tomorrow, or I suspect I'd be looking for new tenants."

George walked a few steps away from Rachel and then turned to
look back. "Do you really need tenants, Rachel? Seems like you've
got a pretty full house as it is." He stood with hands jammed in his
pockets and feet spread wide.

Rachel felt as though she'd been attacked, and all her training in
the courtroom flooded over her. Before she could restrain herself,
she launched back at him. "You don't know what you're getting
yourself into, George. Belle and Mary are more than photographs."
And she turned her back and marched up to the house. When she
slammed the kitchen door behind herself, the loud bang brought her
back to her senses.

Where did that come from, she wondered. She turned back to see
if she'd left George standing, or if the anger she felt had shattered the

scene behind her. She expected to see the barn and all the things around it leveled as if by a tornado, but was relieved to see that everything still stood where she had left it. George, however, was nowhere in sight.

Rachel thought about walking back down the hill to apologize for her outburst or calling to leave a message on his answering machine. No, she decided, she'd let things settle, think about it overnight and deal with it tomorrow.

Maybe he hadn't been hurt. Maybe she was being too hard on herself. Maybe the rage she felt inside hadn't been transmitted to him at all. Rachel stopped her instinctual line of defense and sighed. She knew she had acted like a spoiled little girl whose toys had been taken away. She'd apologize tomorrow.

If Belle and George were falling in love, they deserved all the happiness they could give each other. Belle would make a wonderful farmer's wife, and Mary would thrive growing up on a farm.

"What in the world are you thinking about?" Belle asked, interrupting the scene Rachel was busy creating in her mind.

"If you only knew," Rachel said and gave her friend a hug. "If you only knew."

* * *

Rachel woke early the next day and packed before Belle and Mary left their room. She wanted to get back home. Back to John. She was settling the box that contained her grandmother's wedding gown on the back seat when George approached the car.

"Morning," he said. "Getting an early start, I see."

"Yeah. I'd really like to avoid the rush hour traffic around Charlottesville if I can. Hit that stretch of highway at the wrong time, and you can spend hours stuck in bumper-to-bumper traffic."

"I'll remember that when I come."

Rachel looked surprised but said nothing.

"I'm coming up next weekend to see Belle and Mary," he continued.

Rachel closed the back door to her car and leaned against it. "George, I'm sorry about last night. I don't know what came over me. Please accept my apology. I wish you and Belle the very best."

"Sure thing."

The two stood silently. Ralph ran over and licked George's hand.

"Ralph will miss them," Rachel said.

"Wait a minute, lady. You're way ahead of us here. Nobody's going anywhere. Slow down. Slow waaaaay down."

As Rachel tried to slow down – something her father had drilled in her head over and over – she heard the front door slam and a squeal echoed across the yard. "George! George!" Mary sang as she launched herself into the man's arms.

Sure, she thought. Who can resist that? She looked up to the porch and saw Belle beam at her daughter and the man who now held her up to the morning sun.

"Everybody ready to head back home?" Rachel asked, tossing Mary's blanket in the back next to her car seat. George buckled the child in and kissed her on the top of her head. "You be a good girl now. Do what your Mommy tells you, and I'll bring you a surprise when I come," he said.

"Chicken?"

"No chickens in the city. You have to come here for chickens." Everybody laughed as doors were closed and seatbelts fastened. "Call when you get there," George said, leaning in the car's passenger window to give Belle a peck on the cheek.

Rachel turned the key in the ignition and slowly backed the car out of its space beside the house so they were facing down the long driveway. Belle turned to wave one last time. Rachel watched in the rear view mirror as George waved back.

111

"He's a good man," she said finally. She looked over at Belle's face and knew that she agreed.

"He's really good with Mary," the young woman added.

"Yes, but it's obvious he's crazy about you, too. I see the way he looks at you."

Belle sat for a few minutes in silence, as if trying to decide whether to speak.

"What is it, Belle? Something the matter?" Rachel had lots of experience getting clients to trust her with their secrets. Belle chewed on a cuticle for a while. Rachel waited patiently. Waiting was part of the game, and she knew the game well.

"So, Rachel, did you and George ever . . . you know, well . . ."

"Have a thing for each other?"

"I mean, I know it's none of my business, and it really doesn't matter, but . . ."

"Did George say we did?"

"No, but I just wondered. You came up here several times last year, and you're both single, and you're pretty, and he likes you, and he's . . ."

"No, Belle, George and I were never romantically involved. Not to say I don't find him very attractive. You're a mighty lucky girl to have caught his eye. And if John weren't in the picture, it might have been a different story."

Belle settled back into her seat and laid her head against the window. Mary sang softly in the backseat. Finally, the singing stopped, and Rachel realized the child had sung herself to sleep.

"I'll need to tell Ricky that George is coming to see us. I can't leave him dangling, thinking there's some chance we might get back together."

"Take it slow," Rachel cautioned. "Don't burn any bridges. You don't know if this thing with George will work out or not. Long distance romances are hard to sustain."

Belle set her chin and Rachel recognized the look of a determined woman.

"And what about your school? You're doing so well. I'd hate to see you drop out again."

Belle rattled on about online classes and the community college near the farm. Then she stopped herself with a laugh.

"Listen to me. We haven't even had an official date yet, and I've started to pack my bags."

"I know it's tempting to want a knight in shining armor to rescue you from all the challenges of being a single mother," Rachel said. "But believe me, I've seen a whole other set of problems with stepparents, so be careful."

"Look who's talking," Belle laughed. "Isn't that what you're getting ready to do in less than two weeks? Walk down the aisle into the role of Ben's stepmother?"

"Grandmother is more like it, but yes, I am, and I know what's ahead of me. It's not all sweetness, Belle."

Belle looked like she was about to burst into tears, and Rachel realized she'd gone too far. Twice in one morning is too many times for anybody to have to apologize, she thought, but she forged ahead. "Belle, I'm sorry. You're a grown woman. I'm sure you know what you're doing. I just want you to be happy."

Belle sniffled and let Rachel pat her hand.

"Here, have a cookie," Rachel said, rooting around in the paper bag between them. "I forgot them on the way up. They're probably a little stale, but they're still chocolate."

"Don't eat too many of these, or you won't be able to fit in that dress," Belle warned, turning the conversation from herself and on to the upcoming wedding. Rachel moaned.

"I'm too old for this," she said. "Too old and too mean. What in the world am I getting myself into?"

Belle took her turn and patted Rachel's hand on the steering wheel. "On the other hand, maybe you need another," she said and handed the older woman a second cookie.

* * *

Rachel knew something was wrong as soon as she walked through the front door. The house was too quiet. Instead of rushing to his water bowl, Ralph dashed up the stairs.

"We're up here, Rachel," John called from above her.

Rachel dropped her suitcase and purse on the floor in the hall and ran up the steps to Ben's room, where she found Ralph furiously licking the child's face. John rose from the rocking chair beside the bed and walked toward her like a man struggling to reach the surface from the bottom of very deep water. He clung to her like a life preserver.

"I've got a call in to the doctor to see whether I should take him in. We've been up all night. He's got a pretty high fever."

Rachel leaned over and kissed Ben's forehead. Her lips felt like they'd been seared by a hot iron. She whispered so as not to wake the sleeping boy. "Any other symptoms?"

John shook his head. "We went to the video arcade and played games for about an hour, and then he started complaining that his head hurt so we left. I took his temperature as soon as we got home. It was 103 degrees. I gave him some aspirin and he cooled off pretty quick. Kept him quiet the rest of the day. He didn't want to eat, and I didn't force him. I did get him to drink a little juice, but that's about it."

"You don't look so good, yourself," Rachel said. "Why don't you go lie down for a while and let me take over. I'll wake you up when the doctor calls."

John seemed reluctant to leave Ben's side. "Come on, John," Rachel said, "he's sleeping. There's nothing you can do that I can't."

"Maybe we should take him to the emergency room."

"Let's give the doctor another half hour. I'll keep an eye on the temperature in the meantime. Go."

John kissed the child again and then folded Rachel into an embrace that left her breathless. "I'm so glad you're back," he said.

"Me, too."

Ralph licked John's hand as if to assure him that he, too, was glad to be home. Rachel claimed her seat in the now empty rocker and listened to John walk down the hall and into his bedroom. She didn't hear his door close and knew he had left the room but not his job of listening. She hoped he'd be able to doze a little at least. She remembered the toll Mary's hospital stay had taken on Belle and hoped John, a much older parent figure, wouldn't have to go through a long drawn-out siege of fear.

She looked at the flushed face in the bed. Such a dear boy, she thought. She glanced down at the Scooby Doo "marriage ring" he had loaned his grandfather when he suggested a marriage proposal. A faint voice interrupted the memory. "You're back," Ben said.

"Hi, there, big boy. What's going on with you?"

"Granddad missed you," Ben said, ignoring her question.

"I missed your Granddad. And you. So did Ralph."

At the mention of his name, the dog leaped from his post on the other side of the bed and gave another swipe across the child's face. Ben didn't even have the strength to turn his head away. The phone rang, and Rachel dashed into the hall to answer it. She and John collided on the second ring. She let him pick up the receiver.

"Hello, doctor. Thanks for calling back," he said and then launched into the story he had told Rachel just moments before. Then he listened. Minutes ticked by while Rachel waited to hear what was being said on the other end. Finally, John hung up the phone and looked at Rachel.

"She thinks we'd better take him to the hospital. Better to be safe than sorry."

"Of course. Let me go put Ralph out, and I'll be ready."

John didn't argue. His face registered the relief he felt to have her make the trip to the hospital with him. Rachel picked up the phone and called Belle to tell her what was going on.

"If we're gone for very long, let Ralph back in for me, okay?"

"Sure," Belle said. "Anything else we can do?"

Rachel started to say, "Nothing" and then changed her mind. "Pray," she said instead and hung up.

Chapter Thirteen

T he drive to the hospital felt like it lasted an hour instead of 10 minutes. John had wrapped Ben in his favorite blanket and tucked Pooh into his arms. Instead of his usual chatter whenever the family rode in the car, the child lay quietly in the back seat with his head in Rachel's lap. John glanced in the rear view mirror to check on them.

"I can't believe it," he said as they neared the hospital. "There's a parking space."

He whipped the car into place and ran around to open the back door for Rachel. As he leaned in to pick Ben up in his arms, Rachel saw the creases in his brow and the grim line of his mouth.

"I can walk, Granddad," Ben insisted, but when he stepped out on to the curb, he pitched forward. John caught him before he hit the sidewalk and scooped him up. The child began to whimper, and Rachel grabbed one of his hands and squeezed it.

The doctor had called ahead and an emergency team waited at the door to usher them immediately to an examining room. "The doctor will be right with you," a nurse said, giving Rachel a comforting pat on her arm.

"Thanks," John said. He continued to hold Ben on his lap.

"Am I going to die like Mommy and Daddy?" Ben asked from deep within his blanket.

"Of course not, Ben," John said in his best adult voice, but Rachel could tell he was scared. His eyes had sunk deep within their sockets as though he were hiding there from something that terrified him.

117

"You've probably caught some silly bug at school," Rachel said. "The doctor will give you some medicine to kill the bug, and you'll be good as new."

"She won't give me a shot, will she?" Ben asked, starting to cry. "I don't want a shot. They hurt."

"Whatever the doctor says will be the thing you'll need to do to get better," John said. "You'll need to be a big boy, right?"

Ben whimpered and held his Pooh bear close. The doctor walked in before he could ask too many more questions.

"Hi, there, Ben Turner. What's going on here?" Dr. Cox moved confidently into the room, focusing on her patient first, giving him her undivided attention. She acknowledged the adults in the room only after she'd tousled his hair and pinched his nose playfully.

She didn't look much more than a child, herself. Rachel had liked her the minute she'd met her several months before when she first became Ben and Mary's doctor. In her mid-30s, her tomboy look endeared her to the children. She pulled her blonde hair back in a ponytail and sported lime green braces on her teeth. She wore blue jeans and high-top tennis shoes. A red bandanna tied around her neck completed the ensemble.

"Let's check this guy's temperature first," she said, whipping out a digital thermometer and zooming it into his mouth like an airplane. Rachel watched as she wrote down an alarming "105."

"Okay," she muttered. "Any symptoms since we spoke on the phone?"

"He vomited," John said.

Dr. Cox nodded her head and scribbled on his chart. She patted Ben's knee. "Let's take a look inside your mouth, big boy." Ben opened his mouth, and she poked around thoroughly. Looked in his ears, shined a light in his eyes, listened to his chest with her stethoscope, felt his stomach and thumped around his back.

"I think we'll need to run some tests," she said, directing her attention toward John and Rachel. "I'm going to admit him." Her voice was firm and Rachel realized nobody would question the young doctor's authority.

"Is this the hospital Mary went to?" Ben whined.

"Yes," John said. "Remember how nice everybody was to Mary?"

When Ben started to cry, Rachel sat down on the examining table next to him.

"I don't want to stay here," he shrieked. "I can't leave Ralph. I'll be all alone at night without Ralph."

"No, you won't, Ben," Rachel said. "Your grandfather and I will be right here with you the whole time."

Dr. Cox stepped out of the room and spoke to the nurse. She came back in within minutes. "They'll have a room ready for him in a second." She looked at Ben and said, "A very nice room with a television and lots of pretty nurses."

She asked John to step outside while Rachel stayed with Ben.

"Mr. Turner, I've called in an infectious disease specialist and ordered a lumbar puncture ASAP. A spinal tap will identify for sure, but I suspect that Ben has meningitis. It's caused by a bacteria called *strep pneumoniae*. If I'm right, he's going to be in the hospital for a couple of weeks of treatment.

The spinal tap will show signs of meningitis in the blood, white cells and glucose. A culture will identify any resistance to therapy. As soon as we get a positive confirmation of the diagnosis, we'll start treatment."

"How long will that take?" John asked.

"A couple of hours. I'll tell you more when I see you later today. Let's take this a step at a time." She patted John on the shoulder as if he were the child.

When John and Dr. Cox walked back into the examining room, Ben's face was buried in Pooh's fur. Dr. Cox ruffled his hair and smiled at Rachel.

"Everybody here has my orders. They'll proceed accordingly, and I'll be by to check on things later this evening. He's going to be well taken care of. You all take care of each other."

Rachel and John looked at each other over Ben's head. Rachel took a deep breath and let it out in a long, slow exhale. John did the same.

* * *

A young nurse helped Ben into his hospital gown. A mild sedative prepared him for the procedure.

"Looks like you guys could use one of these, too," she said. "Relax. He's in good hands. Dr. Foreman is one of the best ID doctors in DC. He and Dr. Cox will get this little guy taken care of and on the road to recovery before you know it."

John and Rachel stood on opposite sides of Ben's bed, waiting for the doctor to arrive to administer the spinal tap.

"Do you know anything about meningitis?" John whispered to Rachel, careful not to wake Ben.

"I think it's pretty serious, John."

"How serious?"

Rachel was afraid to share what she'd learned over the years. She knew that if it wasn't caught in time, it could result in hearing loss. Worse, yet, children died. In the sub-Sahara region, it was endemic.

"Let's wait to see what the doctor tells us, John. Stay in the moment. We don't really know anything yet."

The door opened, and a tall, gray-haired doctor bustled in with two nurses trailing behind him with equipment. Without making eye contact, Dr. Foreman introduced himself and moved to Ben's bed. The child barely opened his eyes and allowed himself to be turned on his side without the least resistance. His lethargy worried Rachel.

She wished he would put up a fight. She wished he'd do anything rather than lie there.

She turned her head at the sight of the long needle and didn't turn around again until she heard the doctor prepare to leave the room. What she saw took her breath away. John looked like all his life had been sucked out of him.

Ben lay flat under the hospital sheets. An IV had been inserted in his arm and snaked up to three plastic bags hanging above him.

"I've started him on dexamethasone, an anti-inflammatory drug to prevent any neurological damage, and two antibiotics, varcomycin and ceftrioxone. We'll be able to confirm the diagnosis shortly and hopefully this treatment will work. Any questions?"

John and Rachel were too stunned to reply. Each shook their heads.

"Dr. Cox will be by later. I'll be back tomorrow. Let the nurses know if you need anything."

One of the nurses left with the doctor. The other, an older woman who looked like she'd seen her share of illness, smiled and smoothed Ben's hair back from his eyes.

"Poor little tyke," she said. "It's been a rough ride, hasn't it? Rest now, my sweet. Rest well."

She turned to John and offered her hand. "I'm Nancy, Mr. Turner. You did a good thing by getting him in here so quickly."

"Did I? Maybe I should have brought him last night when he first got sick."

"Don't second-guess yourself, Mr. Turner. You did fine. Rest now. We'll be back to check on him in a few minutes. Call if you need us."

"Thanks," Rachel said, speaking the word John was too dazed to get out of his mouth.

After the nurse left, Rachel walked around to John's side of the bed and placed her hand on top of his, where it lay on Ben's little chest. They watched as their two hands rose and fell with each breath.

"I guess I should go back to the house and get his things," Rachel said. "Looks like he'll be here for some time."

"Do you mind?" John asked. "Or I could go."

"No, you stay here. You should be here when he wakes up. I'll be back soon. I'll just make a few phone calls while I'm there. Anyone you want me to call for you?"

John asked her to call his secretary to tell her what was going on. His partner on the project would need to know he'd probably be away from work for several days.

"I'll grab your shaving kit, too," Rachel said. "Anything else you need?"

John shook his head. "Thanks, Rachel. What would I have done without you to go through this with me?"

Rachel smiled. "I don't know, John, but I'm sure glad, too."

* * *

Before Rachel opened her front door, she heard Susan's voice. "Rachel, what's going on?" her friend yelled, running across the street. "I saw you all leaving. What's wrong with Ben? What happened? Where is he?"

Rachel opened the door and pulled her friend inside. "Hush, Susan. I don't want the whole neighborhood upset."

The phone rang just as a knock sounded on the back door. Rachel opened it to find Belle and Mary standing on the back stoop. "Come on in," Rachel said picking up the phone. Mrs. Moser was on the other end. Rachel didn't wait for her to ask the question.

"Ben's in the hospital. John's with him. I'm here to pick up a few things. They're running tests, but they're pretty sure it's meningitis, and that he'll get through it okay. He's got good doctors."

Mrs. Moser asked for details, but Rachel put on her lawyer attitude and cut the call short. "I'll let you know when we know something. Thanks for calling."

As soon as she hung up, the phone rang again. Rachel ignored it.

"Oh, Rachel, you must be worried sick," Susan wailed. "And the wedding only two weeks away. What will we do?"

"WE won't do anything, Susan. I'M going back to the hospital to be with John and Ben. YOU can take care of Ralph if you will."

"Of course, I'll take care of Ralph. Maybe I should go back with you. Do you want me to ride back to the hospital with you? Maybe I should drive."

"I'll take a cab, Susan. Belle, would you call Ben's teacher and let her know what's going on?"

"Sure."

"Where's Ben?" Mary asked. "Where's Ben gone?"

"Ben will be back soon, honey," her mother said. But the little girl wasn't satisfied until she got an answer to her question. When Belle finally told her that Ben was sick and had to go to the hospital, the child's face lit up.

"Balloons," she squealed. "Balloons for Ben"

Rachel laughed. "Thanks, Mary. That's a great idea." She made a mental note to buy some balloons on her way back to the hospital and then placed calls to Georgia and John's office. Both conversations were short and to the point. She promised to call again when she had more news. Georgia promised to bring cookies that night.

When Rachel walked into Ben's room to pack his pajamas and toothbrush, reality hit her. Meningitis killed. Ben might not make it. He might not ever sleep in the little room she had fixed up especially for him. She remembered the day he and John had moved their things upstairs from the basement apartment John had rented. Rachel had let Ben arrange his toys in the closet all by himself. Her eyes filled with tears at the memory of his excitement when he ran down the stairs to get her to come see his work.

Rachel grabbed the things she needed from his room and ran to retrieve John's shaving kit. Tears blinded her, and she stumbled in the hallway. Susan heard the clatter from downstairs and called up to her.

"Rachel, are you okay?"

"Sure, I'm fine," she answered, but she knew the words were a lie.

Chapter Fourteen

When Rachel returned to Ben's hospital room an hour later, John stood outside the door. Leaning up against the wall, he looked like a man facing a firing squad. He didn't glance up until Rachel stood directly in front of him. The eyes that met hers lay dull and glassy in their sockets.

"Ben just threw up again," he said. "They're in there now cleaning him up. They've given him something for the nausea. He's still complaining of a headache and a stiff neck."

Rachel wrapped her arms around John and leaned her head against his chest. They stood there together until the two nurses came out with the soiled linen and told them they could go back in the hospital room. Ben was already asleep again when they approached his bedside.

Rachel tied the balloons to the end of the bed so he'd see them as soon as he opened his eyes. "How are you holding up?" she whispered.

John nodded his head but didn't answer.

"Can I bring you something to eat from the cafeteria? Georgia's coming over later with cookies, but you need some supper first."

John shook his head. "He asked for Ralph," he finally said. "He said he needed Ralph to make him well. He really missed him while you were at the farm."

Rachel felt guilt wring her heart like a giant vise. She didn't know what to say.

John seemed to feel her recoil and reached out to touch her for the first time. "Sorry, I didn't mean to hurt you. Didn't mean that to come out the way it did. Forgive me?"

"Nothing to forgive. Don't worry. I'm a big girl, remember."

"That's what I love about you," John said, but he continued to hold her hand.

"Horace's funeral is tomorrow," Rachel said. "I'm trying to decide what to do. I feel like I should go, but I don't want to leave you here by yourself."

John looked like he'd just been told he had to face an army alone. Rachel watched as he fought with his inner demons.

"The nurses said tonight should be a turning point," he said. "The antibiotics they're giving him should start making a difference, and he could be feeling lots better by tomorrow. Or worse if the culture shows it's a strain that is resistant to the drugs they're giving him."

Rachel took a minute to let that information sink in. She tried to detach from the actual person involved and examine the facts as though she had been handed a medical file in a case she was working on. She was mildly successful.

"I'll decide tomorrow," she said. "The funeral's at 11 o'clock. Let's see how he gets along tonight and what the morning looks like. Fair?"

John nodded his head.

Ben stirred, and Rachel moved closer to the bed so he'd know she was with him as soon as he woke. When his eyes opened, the first things they focused on were the balloons. A smile spread across his face but faded quickly as the pains in his head and neck attacked.

"When can I go home?" he whimpered. "Hospitals make me sick."

John laughed and stepped forward to stand on the other side of the bed. "Well, hospitals don't make you sick. They're where you go when you ARE sick to get well. You'll be here today, that's all we know right now. Okay? Just today, and Rachel and I are right here with you."

"And me, too," Dr. Cox chimed in. She wore the red bandana over her nose like a bandit, which got a weak chuckle from Ben. "How you doing pardner?"

"I want to go home," the child moaned, more forcefully than his initial request. The one-day-at-a-time approach hadn't fooled him at all.

"That's what everybody says," the young woman pouted. "Nobody likes it here. Nobody wants to stay with me."

Ben smiled but didn't seem to be able to muster the strength for a comeback. Dr. Cox consulted the clipboard at the bottom of the bed and made a few notes on it. She turned her attention to the adults in the room. "The results of the spinal tap verified my suspicions. Ben has meningitis. We'll continue the treatment we've started him on and hope it works. The next couple of days are critical. We should see an improvement by Monday. I hope."

Rachel and John looked at each other, trying to be strong for the other. "So, we wait," Rachel said.

"We wait," Dr. Cox repeated. "We're doing everything we can at this point. He's a strong, healthy little boy, and he's surrounded by the best medicine in the world. Love."

Rachel looked at the child in the bed and the man hovering over him and felt a pain in her chest. Her heart was full of love and full of fear. She wondered which would win.

"I'm right at the other end of the phone line if anybody needs me," Dr. Cox said. "You two take turns going home to rest. You need to stay healthy for Ben's sake."

John and Rachel nodded, but each knew they wouldn't leave the other alone until the crisis had passed.

* * *

When Georgia knocked on the door to Ben's room later that evening and didn't get a response, her heart skipped a beat. She stood in the hall, running several equally terrifying scenarios through her mind before she finally pushed the door open and poked her head around it. All three occupants of the room were asleep. Ben lay in the bed, while Rachel curled beside John in the recliner.

Georgia tiptoed in with her plate of cookies and placed them on the ledge under the window. Rachel opened her eyes and sat straight up, waking John in the process.

"Sorry to wake you," Georgia said. "How are things going?"

Rachel looked over at Ben. "The doctor verified the diagnosis. Meningitis. He's being treated. Now we wait."

Georgia nodded. Having recently gone through a cancer scare with her husband, she was all too familiar with hospitals and waiting. "How are you two doing?" she asked, although she knew the answer when she looked at their faces.

"I'm mighty glad to have Rachel home," John said. "I don't know how I'd get through this without her."

Rachel tried to look stoic, but her friend had known her long enough to recognize the fear underneath the straight spine.

"How are things at the office?" Rachel asked, diverting attention to more manageable affairs. Things she could control were so much easier to handle.

"Lots of calls about Horace. Everything else is quiet. I don't guess you'll get to the funeral."

Rachel glanced over at John. "We'll wait to see what happens tonight," she said. "I'll call you tomorrow morning and let you know. You're going, right?"

Georgia said she would attend the funeral and that she had scheduled a meeting to go over the will with his family. The probate ball was already rolling.

One more time, Rachel reminded herself how lucky she was to have Georgia. Now, if she could only fix Ben.

"Anything else you need me to do?" Georgia asked, thinking of all the wedding plans but knowing not to bring them up yet.

Susan was another story. Just as Georgia had the question out of her mouth, the door burst open and with hurricane force, Susan swept in.

"This is just the most horrible timing," she said breathlessly. "Children and their bugs. Always right at the worst possible times. I remember the year both of mine came down with the measles right when we'd planned . . ."

"Susan, Ben has meningitis," Rachel said, interrupting her friend's torrent before John choked her. Susan slumped down dramatically in the one empty chair in the room.

"Oh, you poor dears," she gasped. "How can you stand it?" And then getting right back on track, she charged forward. "Do you want me to cancel the wedding?"

Rachel looked at John to gauge how well he was handling Susan's take-charge attitude. He seemed to be managing. Perhaps better than she was. She felt herself about to erupt and was able to control herself only because she knew how much Susan loved Ben.

"Susan, thanks, but we really can't even think about the wedding right now."

"But the cake lady . . ."

"Here, Susan, have a cookie," Georgia chimed in, interrupting a litany of things Susan was about to list that needed to be done. "We've got plenty of time to think about the wedding next week. After Ben is well on his way to recovery."

Susan looked chastened, but she was no match for Georgia's protectiveness of Rachel, and she knew it. She rose from the chair and tiptoed to the bed. From her purse, she pulled out a get-well card and a coloring book and crayons.

"I bought him these the last time I babysat," she said. "He really loves to color." She patted the Scooby Doo picture on the cover, for the first time registering the seriousness of the situation in front of her. "Oh, sweetie," she said, gently touching Ben's face. "Get well soon. I miss you across the street. I don't have anybody to play with me."

"How was your weekend away with Jim?" Rachel asked. "Did you guys have fun?"

"It was like a second honeymoon," Susan said. "I wish we'd done it a long time ago. It's what we needed. To get away alone."

"Guess it took what it took," Rachel said. "It happened when it happened. Things usually do."

* * *

Rachel and John took turns stretching out on the cot throughout the long night. Nurses rushed in and out, checking on Ben. His temperature continued to rise and fall, but the nausea eased off in the early morning hours. Ben slept more than either of the adults in the room.

Sometime in the endless night, Rachel looked over at John. He had taken his turn on the recliner and stared at his grandson as if willing him to get well.

"It's hard, isn't it?" she said.

"The hardest thing I've ever had to go through," he said, "bar none. His parents' death was so sudden. So final. This waiting and knowing there's nothing I can do is agony, Rachel."

Rachel propped herself up on her elbows and nodded. "Well, you're doing a good job at what you do best," she said. "You're loving him."

A young nurse, who didn't look old enough to wear the uniform, bustled in and changed the IV bags. She jotted something on the chart at the end of the bed and bustled back out.

"Want to switch places?" Rachel asked. "I'm awake anyway. I might as well sit."

John agreed to lie down for the rest of the night while Rachel took the post beside Ben's bed. She reached out and held the boy's hand, marveling at how much bigger it had gotten in the short time she'd known him. His voice surprised her.

"Rachel?"

"Yes, Ben."

"Can Ralph come see me?"

"I don't think they allow dogs in hospitals, Ben."

"Why not?"

"Animals carry germs, and hospitals are full of sick people. We wouldn't want Ralph to make somebody sicker, would we?"

"Ralph doesn't have germs. We give him a bath."

"I know that, honey, but if they let us bring our dog in, all the other children would want to bring their dogs in, too. And cats and horses and snakes."

"No snakes," Ben said. "And no bugs."

"See all the problems we'd cause if we brought Ralph to visit you?"

Ben turned his face away, and Rachel saw the tears spill over. She wiped his cheeks with a tissue from the box on the bedside table.

"I can't get well without Ralph," the child suddenly shrieked. "I'm going to get worser and worser. Only Ralph can help me."

John sat up and rushed to the bedside. "What's going on? What's the matter?" he asked.

"He wants Ralph," Rachel whispered. The sobs coming from the bed grew louder and louder. A nurse passing by the door heard the noise and stepped into the room.

"What's the problem here?" she asked in an efficient take-charge tone of voice.

"Not sure it's a problem you can do anything about unless you can get permission for us to bring our dog over here. Ben wants to see him."

"Now, Ben, you know we can't do that," the nurse said, "but you'll be going home soon, and you'll see him then."

Ben's wails grew louder. The nurse left the room and returned with a hypodermic needle full of something that quieted the boy. He quickly drifted back to sleep, tears drying on his face.

"Can I have one of those, too?" John joked.

"Make that two," Rachel said. "I don't think we've heard the last of the Ralph request."

Chapter Fifteen

S usan called Rachel's cellphone early Friday morning. Rachel answered it on the first ring, hoping that it wouldn't wake Ben. She walked out into the hall and stepped outside to the patio where cellphone conversations were allowed.

"How was the night?" Susan asked as soon as Rachel could talk.

"Pretty good. Ben slept better than John and I did, I'm sure." She told Susan about Ben's crying fit when he was told Ralph couldn't come see him in the hospital. Susan had as much trouble accepting the news as Ben.

"Well, can't the doctor get the rules bent just this once? Don't you know someone on the board who can pull a few strings? I mean, really. Maybe, Jim . . ."

"Stop, Susan. We're not going to have Ralph here in the hospital. Ben needs to learn about rules. That they apply to everyone, including him. This is as good a time as any to learn that lesson."

"No, it's not. He's sick," Susan insisted. And then, as if she had come to some place in her mind where she had crossed over a hurdle only she could see, she abruptly changed the subject. "Are you going to Horace's funeral?"

"I think I will. Ben seems to be stable, and John has encouraged me to go ahead and leave."

Susan said she would stop by the hospital while Rachel was gone.

"Thanks, Susan. Maybe you can take Ben's mind off Ralph."

"Maybe," Susan said and hung up.

Rachel spoke to several other family members enjoying the fresh air on the patio and then hurried back inside to Ben's room. When she walked in, the young Asian man they had met the night before was arranging the breakfast tray so Ben could reach everything.

"My goodness," Rachel said. "Don't you ever leave?"

"Working a double shift," he said. "We've got a bunch of people out this week." He lifted the lid off the plate and put it on the window ledge. "Afraid there's not much here to tempt a kid, but until we're sure his stomach has settled, this is about all he'll get. Get well soon, Ben, and I promise something a little more exciting, okay?"

Ben surveyed the tray in front of him and stuck out his bottom lip.

"Come on, Ben, let's see what we've got here," John said. "You need to get your strength back, you know."

Rachel told herself this would be a good time to leave. She'd never had much luck getting children to eat, even when they were healthy. "John, the funeral's at eleven o'clock. I should be back by one, at least. Susan said she's planning to stop by while I'm gone. Why don't you take that opportunity to run home and rest for awhile."

Ben whimpered. "I'll be all by myself. Don't go, Granddaddy."

John looked at Rachel and shrugged his shoulders. "Don't worry, Ben. I won't leave you. I'll be right here."

"And I'll be back as soon as I can," Rachel said, sealing her promise to both with a kiss.

* * *

Horace Gilbert's funeral was the spectacle Rachel had expected. Limos lined the street in front of the Washington Cathedral, the church where Horace and his family had sat in the same pew for decades.

Rachel found Georgia seated near the back and eased into the pew next to her. The two blew air kisses at each other and settled into comfortable silence. Horace's staff was seated behind the large section reserved for family. Rachel had declined the invitation to sit with them, preferring the anonymity of a back row with Georgia.

She noticed Horace's latest secretary perched at one end of a pew, dabbing at her eyes. The young woman wore a black pillbox hat with a veil, but Rachel could still see the mascara smeared on her cheeks. Horace always had a way with women, Rachel thought. Even after years of women's lib, no matter how badly he degraded them, they still loved his big daddy bear gruffness. His secretary wasn't the only woman crying. Rachel saw several former employees scattered throughout the church. They might have quit working for him, but, in their hearts, they never completely left him.

When the family entered, Carrie walked down the aisle, holding on to Horace Junior's arm. She was accompanied by an elderly lady.

"Any idea who that is with Carrie?" Georgia whispered.

"Not sure, but it may be her grandmother," Rachel said. "I know they're very close, and she lives here in DC. Carrie's parents are retired and have a home somewhere in Florida, I think."

The family seated themselves, followed by the many rows of people behind them.

"Carrie knows to come to the reading of the will, right?" Rachel whispered to her secretary. Georgia nodded and fanned herself with the program. "I've got it scheduled in our office tomorrow at three o'clock. The conference room will be crowded, but it shouldn't take long."

Rachel nodded, and the two bowed their heads as the distinguished looking minister welcomed the congregation. Several men Horace's age marched to the pulpit to eulogize the man they had both hated and admired in their long careers doing business with him. Rachel smiled as she recognized one of the men who had sat on the opposite side of the bargaining table more than once. Death certainly levels the playing field, she thought.

The last speaker was a small elderly black woman who could barely see over the pulpit. She wore a flowered house dress, white tennis shoes and a straw sun bonnet. She had worked as Horace's housekeeper for more than 40 years.

"Mr. Horace was a good man," she said in a voice that boomed out across the sea of white faces. "He was a mighty good man to me and to my family. Paid me right up to the day he died, even though I ain't been worth much since the arthritis set in."

A murmur swept through the crowd. Rachel imagined the surprise people felt at such generosity. Horace was known as a tight man. He insisted on getting more than his money's worth and had been accused more than once of cheating his employees.

"Both my boys got their college learning because of Mr. Horace," she continued, "and I owe him for that. He's in heaven now. Up in heaven with his Lord."

As the tiny figure hobbled back to her seat with the family, the church grew quiet, as though all the sound had been sucked dry by the woman's last words. Words that were so full of heart compared to the Rotarians who had spoken before her.

Rachel watched as several people in front of her wiped tears from their faces, something she hadn't expected to see at this funeral. She and Georgia looked at each other and shook their heads.

* * *

When Rachel returned to the hospital, the laughter coming from Ben's room shocked her.

"What's going on?" she asked as she passed by the nurses' station.

"Your cousin and her seeing-eye dog are visiting Ben," the young woman behind the desk said with a smile. "Best medicine he's had so far."

"My cousin?" Rachel stopped herself from saying she didn't have a blind cousin. Even before she opened the door and walked into Ben's room, she knew what had happened.

Susan wore dark glasses and held Ralph's harness, allowing him close enough to Ben's bed so the boy could reach him but not giving the dog enough leash so he could jump in the bed.

Ben's face was all smiles. "Look, Rachel, it's Ralph. Susan brought Ralph here to make me well."

"I see she did," Rachel said through clinched teeth. She looked at John to gauge his reaction to Susan's manipulation of the rules. Susan recognized her friend's expression and rose to leave. "Well, guess Ralph and I should get on home, Ben. Can't stay too long. You know how dogs are. Gotta get outside. Gotta run."

"Thanks, Susan. You're the best. I feel all well already. Bye, Ralph. I'll be home soon."

Susan patted John on the way out the door but ducked past Rachel without a word.

"Be careful, cousin, that your negative karma doesn't catch up to you," Rachel said. "They tell me being blind isn't something you'd handle very well. Sure would hate for you to have to depend on a seeing-eye dog in your next life."

Susan huffed out of the room without looking back and closed the door firmly. "Your cousin is amazing the way she gets around," said the young nurse who came in behind her.

"Yes, isn't she," Rachel said. "And you should see her tap dance. It's truly a miracle."

* * *

Rachel's conference room was full to overflowing a good fifteen minutes before the appointed hour of three o'clock.

"The vultures have swarmed," Georgia muttered under her

breath when Rachel returned from a one o'clock real estate closing. She handed over the file. "Need a cup of coffee?"

"I probably need something stronger than that," Rachel answered, sitting down in the rocking chair near Georgia.

"How about a cookie?" her secretary asked, offering one from the plate she kept on the corner of her desk.

"Aaaah, chocolate," Rachel moaned, consuming the cookie in two huge bites. Wiping crumbs from her mouth and the front of her black linen jacket, she stood up, squared her shoulders and marched toward the closed conference room door as if she were going into battle. All eyes turned in her direction when she stepped to the table.

"Good afternoon," she began. "Thanks for being here. I know some of you have busy schedules and flights to catch, so I'll try to make this quick. Horace spent a lifetime working to create an empire that wasn't always easy to manage, so it may surprise you that his will is relatively simple and straight forward."

Rachel opened the file and removed the document bound in the usual blue cover. She saw the look of surprise on the faces in front of her as its thin size registered on them. She knew they must have expected a document as thick as the DC phone book.

"Let me begin," she said, reading slowly and clearly. "To my wife, I leave our homes in Georgetown, Pawley's Island, Manhattan and Paris, as well as a monthly income of $100,000 to support her as long as she lives." Rachel looked up at the widow. "There is also a letter here for you," she said, handing it to the woman who appeared to be heavily drugged.

She nodded and took the envelope.

"To my children, Horace Junior and Mildred, I leave $1 million each." Rachel did not look up to see how the two reacted. She knew they would be disappointed.

"To my faithful employee, Bertha Williams, I leave $50,000."

A gasp broke the silence in the room. Rachel looked up at the shriveled black woman. She was the only one in the room smiling.

"God bless you, Mr. Horace," she murmured, rocking back and forth in her chair.

"Finally, to Carrie Johnson, I leave The Gilbert Companies, the business I have worked all my life to grow. I know you will take care of it. You have your grandfather's genes, and you will do well."

At that news, the room erupted. Rachel permitted the outburst to run its course and then rapped on the table for attention. She turned to Carrie, who looked like she had been injected with a drug that made her see creatures that weren't in the room. Wonder and fear crossed her face in flutters of emotion. The looks Horace's children aimed at her were simpler. Hatred.

"I will cut checks from the estate as soon as it is probated," Rachel said. "Carrie, I'll need to speak to you in private for a moment. The rest of you are free to leave." Rachel stood, indicating that the meeting was over. Softening a little, she said, "Horace Gilbert was my client for many years. I grew to consider him as a friend. He wasn't always easy to deal with, but I learned a lot from our relationship."

Horace's widow stifled a sob. She was helped from the room by her son and daughter, one on each side of her. The maid trailed behind. Rachel heard the door to the office open and shut, leaving her alone with Carrie.

"Come on in my office where we can be more comfortable," she said. "Can I get you a drink? Some tea, perhaps?"

"I'd love that," Carrie said.

In her usual way of anticipating the needs of others, Georgia met them in Rachel's office, teapot in hand. She smiled at Carrie and patted her arm. "You doing okay?" she asked.

"I just don't understand this at all," the young woman said, sinking down in one of the chairs near Rachel's desk. "Why me?"

"I believe this letter will explain it all," Rachel said.

Carrie ripped open the envelope and took out a single sheet of paper. Putting on her glasses, she began to read silently.

"Dear Carrie, if you're reading this, I am dead. As you and everyone else in the room with you today knows, I never thought it would happen. I thought I could beat the Grim Reaper, just like I beat everyone else. Guess not. Carrie, I would never have gotten where I did in life without the inspiration and devotion of your grandfather. He believed in me when nobody else did. He funded my college education – or at least tried to. Against his advice, I dropped out to make my fortune other ways. But he never turned his back on me or told me I had done the wrong thing by changing course. Your grandfather was always my greatest supporter in every way. I watched him work on his inventions and never give up and learned to apply that principle in my own line of work. You have his same strength. Take my business now and continue to make it grow. Your friend, Horace Gilbert."

Carrie wiped tears from her cheeks as she folded the letter back into its envelope. She sat with it in her lap for a few minutes of silence. Finally, she looked up at the two women watching her, waiting to see her reaction.

"Now what?" she asked.

"Give yourself a few days to let this sink in. Give yourself as much time as you need. Horace has a great staff of people who are entirely capable of running the business on their own. You'll need to decide at some point whether you want to play an active role or not, and if you do want to be involved, you'll need to decide what to do about your existing job. In the meantime, I have some papers I need you to sign."

Rachel opened a file and passed several documents across the desk, along with a pen. Carrie scanned them briefly and signed where Georgia had stuck red arrows.

Rachel glanced at her watch. "I want to get back to the hospital.

Ben has been sick, and I need to relieve John."

Carrie jumped up and gathered her things. "Yes, I'm so sorry. I had heard, but with all that's been going on, I forgot to ask. How is he?"

"Much better, thanks. We hope he'll come home in a week or so."

"And thanks, too, for your letter recommending another attorney for my case. With all that's happening now, I'm not sure I'll even pursue it."

"Right, and you've got a wedding coming up, I believe."

A dark cloud seemed to pass over Carrie's face. "I hope so. But the way things went today, I'm not so sure."

Rachel thought about the shock that Horace Junior must have felt when he heard his father had left the business to his fiance instead of him. She nodded her head.

"Let me know if you need help," she said.

Carrie thanked her, grabbed a chocolate chip cookie and ducked out the door.

Chapter Sixteen

R achel heard laughter as she walked toward Ben's room. When she opened the door, she saw Mary leaned back on the pillow next to Ben. The two watched cartoons as John dozed in the recliner. He woke when Rachel leaned over and kissed him.

"How did things go?" he asked.

"It's over. Some left happy. Some left mad. Some left totally caught off balance. Your usual reading of a will. How are things here? Where's Belle?"

"She walked down to the cafeteria to get coffee and make some phone calls. She should be back in a minute. She's been gone quite a while."

Ben started to bounce along with one of the cartoon characters, and Rachel rushed to the bed to restrain him. She reached his side just in time to prevent him from pulling an IV loose. He stuck his lower lip out but did as he was told. The better he felt physically, the harder it became to confine him to his bed.

When Belle walked in, Rachel's first question was, "How in the world did you do it?"

"Do what?"

"Keep Mary quiet?"

"Considering all we'd been through before she got sick, it really didn't feel like much of a challenge," Belle laughed.

"Thanks for putting things in perspective," John chimed in. "That always helps."

Belle scooped Mary out of the bed. "Getting little Miss

Squirmbug out of here might help, too. Come on, Mary. Time to go home and check on Ralph." Belle gathered up the coloring books and crayons and placed them on a table with Ben's store of books and goodies.

"Everything okay at home?" Rachel asked.

"Everything's fine. George is coming next weekend, and I need to talk to Ricky. I'm hoping Ricky will spend some time with Mary so George and I can be alone a little." Belle's brow furrowed, and her eyes focused somewhere far away and very dark.

Rachel patted her shoulder. "All is well," she said.

"Yeah, I'm trying to stay in the moment like you taught me, but it's hard. Real hard."

Rachel smiled. "I know. It takes lots of practice. Sitting on the meditation cushion helps. Have you been using mine at all, like I suggested?"

"A little, but I keep forgetting. Maybe when Ben gets home and things settle down again, we can sit together?"

"Sure," Rachel said, "when – if – things settle down." Her mind, her monkey mind, darted to thoughts of the wedding. She knew she'd have to focus on it at some point. Either go ahead with the current plan, postpone it – or cancel it completely.

* * *

Rachel returned home in the daylight and decided to take the opportunity to walk Ralph. Several days had passed since she'd gotten what she called her "Circle fix."

"Come on, boy. Let's go see Deejee," she called out as she gathered his leash and a plastic bag for scooping if he felt the urge to relieve himself during the walk.

Dupont Circle always provided many opportunities. Exercise and fresh air were only two of them. A significant portion of the homeless population of Washington, D.C. congregated there and seeing them always helped Rachel put perspective on her own life. If she felt less than grateful, a trip down the street to mingle with this part of her world always sent her home with a long list of things to be thankful for. Mothers with children always hurt her most deeply, and, as she lost patience with Ben's restlessness, she knew she needed a dose of reality to help remember their own good fortune.

And most especially, each trip to Dupont Circle gave her the opportunity to see the healing power of love. Ralph's fan club hung out at the Circle. He spent his time there moving from one heap of rags to the next, licking, wagging his tail and bringing smiles to the faces of all he met. Ralph loved each person. And he had proved to be a powerful introduction to the sense of community Rachel had never known before.

Deejee, the hotdog vendor, had become one of her best friends after the day Ralph ran off with some of her inventory. The woman lounged in a beach chair under the shade of her umbrella when Rachel walked over.

"How's Ben today?" Deejee asked.

"Ben is feeling so good that he's driving everyone nuts. Surely, they'll let him come home soon, and we can get our lives back. This is one of the hardest things I've ever had to do. I'm just not sure I'm cut out for family life, Deejee."

Rachel said it jokingly, but Deejee knew from the way she tensed her jaw that her friend was seriously concerned about the "in sickness and health" commitment she was about to make.

"Sounds like you're feeling what anybody in your shoes would feel. How about a dog? That'll make you feel better."

Rachel laughed. "All the way. Heavy on the onions."

"Thatta girl," Deejee said as she reached into the steamer with her tongs. "Hey, what's up with Belle and Ricky these days? I've seen them a few times recently with Mary, and they looked like a little family again. Then today he showed up, waited around for awhile and then left, looking like he'd been stood up. Didn't look like a happy camper, I gotta tell you."

"I'm sorry to hear that. Doesn't sound like Belle to stand somebody up. Maybe she forgot to tell him she was going to the hospital."

Rachel considered telling her friend about George but thought better of it. That was Belle's story to tell. A man in a business suit walked over to order a hotdog, saving Rachel from further temptation. Then Ralph ran toward the group, barking loudly.

"What is it, boy?" Ralph trotted over to the entrance to the metro where Rachel saw a girl with a familiar pink Mohawk. She sat with her head resting on her knees. "Well, hello Chelsea," she said as Ralph licked the girl's legs, finally rousing her. She lifted her face and tried to focus on the woman and dog standing in front of her. She didn't say anything for so long Rachel began to wonder if she recognized them.

"Oh, hi," the girl said from what sounded like the bottom of a very deep pit.

"Hi, to you. How're you doing? Everything okay? You don't look too good."

Chelsea stared. Ralph licked her face and then looked at Rachel as if to say, "Do something." Rachel sat down beside the girl and waited. Sometimes that's all you can do, she thought.

After what seemed like hours, Chelsea said, "I fucked up." That's all she said, but Rachel knew what she meant without even seeing the fresh needle marks on her arm.

"How can I help you?" Rachel asked, laying her hand on one knee.

Chelsea lapsed back into silence, but Rachel noticed a tear slide down her dirty cheek. They sat side by side without speaking, Ralph lying beside them. Finally, he lay his head down on his paws and fell asleep. Rachel watched him let go and knew she had to do the same thing. With Chelsea. With Belle. With Ben.

* * *

Within minutes of reaching the comfort of home, Rachel realized she had returned to her fear and desire to do something to help Chelsea. As she sat on her cushion in her third floor meditation room, the idea of calling Ricky hit. Rachel forced her mind back to her breaths successfully for about 10 more minutes before she finally gave up.

Downstairs, she called Belle and asked for Ricky's phone number, explaining that she had a friend with an addiction problem and she hoped Ricky might be able to help. At least he could get her to his NA meeting where the help was available.

Before she hung up the phone, Rachel asked Belle if she had told Ricky about George's visit. She didn't mention her conversation with Deejee.

"Not yet," Belle said. "I'll probably wait until some time next week. I don't want Ricky to have to stew about it too long."

Rachel resisted giving any kind of advice. Instead, she said, "Good luck," and hung up to call Ricky. He answered right away, sounding disappointed when Rachel identified herself.

"Oh, hi, Ms. Springer. I thought you might be Belle."

"Sorry. Just me. And I need to ask a favor."

"Sure," Ricky said, his voice brightening. Thirty days sober, he was still getting used to the idea that he could give help instead of always being on the receiving end.

"You know the girl with the pink Mohawk who hangs out at the Circle?"

"Yeah. I've known Chelsea ever since she showed up on the scene. What about her?"

"She's using again. I saw her today, and she's in really bad shape. I was hoping you could get her to one of your meetings."

"Sure, if she wants to go. Can't really drag her there. Won't work if I do. She's got to be willing."

"But you can try, right?"

"Sure," Ricky said. Just as Rachel was about to hang up, he asked about Belle and Mary. "We were supposed to meet today, and she never came. Do you know if something's wrong? I called, but she hasn't called back yet."

Rachel tried to divert his feelings of abandonment with an appeal to his sympathy. "Have you heard that Ben is in the hospital?" she asked.

"Yeah, I did. Sorry. How is the little guy?"

"Better. Belle and Mary stopped by the hospital today to see him. Belle must have forgotten your plans to get together."

"Yeah, but she could have called," Ricky muttered.

Rachel heard the sharp edge of anger in his voice. Again, she reined herself in from getting in the middle, reminding herself she wasn't the lawyer here, paid to offer advice.

"Want me to give Belle a message?"

"Yeah. Tell her . . ." Ricky stopped himself just in time from spewing forth the venom that Rachel knew was there. "Tell her to call me. Please."

Rachel promised she would. She looked down at Ralph, lying at her feet, ears back. "You got it, boy. A storm is brewing, and it's looking fierce. Batten down the hatches and lie low."

Chapter Seventeen

Rachel grabbed a quick bite to eat and headed back to the hospital. She planned to spend the night so John could go home and sleep in his own bed for the first time since Ben had been admitted to the hospital.

Rachel smiled at the thought, grateful that she could help the man she loved so much. She knew she wanted to make life easier for him in any way she could. When she thought of how huge the burden of a sick child would be on a man his age if he were alone, she marveled again at their story and how very right it all felt.

Then why am I having doubts about marrying him, she wondered.

She parked her car, surprised at finding an empty space almost within spitting distance of the front door. She got out and locked the door, shaking her head to clear away any wedding jitters.

The lobby was filled. Early evening was a popular time to visit. An entire Girl Scout troop headed for the elevator just as she arrived. Each girl held a smiley face helium balloon in one hand and a candy bar in the other. Rachel crowded in the elevator with them, squeezed in one corner with the woman she figured must be the den leader.

"Somebody's going to be mighty happy to see you all," Rachel said. The little girls all turned beaming faces up at her.

"Lily got bit by a dog," a little red-headed, freckle-faced Girl Scout offered. "We're going to make her feel better."

"I'm sure you will," Rachel said, glad the opening of the door cut the conversation short. Mean dog stories always gave her the creeps.

As she walked down the hall toward Ben's room, the name

"Lily" struck her. Surely, not Stan's Lily, she thought. We would have heard something if Stan Berninger's granddaughter were in the same hospital with Ben. Nothing ever went on in the world of Lily that Rachel's private investigator didn't immediately report to everybody he knew.

Still, it wouldn't hurt to ask, so Rachel stopped by the nurse's station and asked for the last name of the child named "Lily" who had been bitten by a dog.

"Sorry, Ms. Springer. I can't give you that information. HIPAA, you know. Privacy regulations."

Rachel felt silly. As a lawyer, she should have known. Guess I'll have to ask Georgia to call Stan to find out, she thought. Or stand out here in the hall and wait to see which room the Girl Scouts come out of.

When Rachel reached Ben's room, she noticed how quiet it seemed, compared to her earlier visit when she found Mary and Ben bounding on the bed together.

The scene had changed dramatically in just a few hours. Ben's face was as white as the sheet and blanket that had been added to keep him warm. "What's wrong?" she asked, rushing across the room to where John sat, crouched over the bed, his hand on Ben's forehead.

"His fever's gone back up," he said. "Things aren't looking good, Rachel."

"What happened? He was feeling so good when I left."

"They think he overdid it. Too much too soon. I shouldn't have let Belle and Mary come. I should . . ."

"Now, wait a minute. Ben's in the hospital being cared for by professionals. Don't take this all on yourself, John."

John didn't look at all relieved by Rachel's reasoning. She put her arms around him and hugged. Still, she could feel the burden he carried, and she knew she couldn't say or do anything to ease it. She pulled up the extra chair and sat with him.

"What does the doctor say?"

"She says the next few hours are critical. They've given him something to help him sleep. Now, we wait. And keep him quiet."

"Guess you won't be going home."

John shook his head and wiped a tear from his cheek. "Thanks, Rachel, for being here with me. I know this isn't the way you planned to spend the days leading up to the wedding. Not much fun. I'm sorry. I wanted everything to be perfect for you."

"Life seldom is, John. Don't worry. This will all be over soon, and our family will be stronger because of the experience, I can promise you."

John looked at Rachel and smiled. As Ben moaned in his sleep, she said a silent prayer that her promise would be kept.

* * *

As soon as she felt comfortable leaving the room, Rachel ducked outside to call Georgia to see if she knew anything about Stan's granddaughter. When Georgia said she didn't, Rachel asked her to call.

"Do you think he knows Ben's in the hospital?" she asked her secretary.

"Stan knows everything. He's a private investigator, remember. That's his job."

"Well, then surely he'll stop by the room and let us know what's going on. In the meantime, give him a buzz, and see what you can find out."

Rachel took a deep breath and hurried back inside. When she told John the dog bite story, he shook his head.

"Children should never have to go through what they do," he said. "I hate it for them. So little," he said, smoothing the hair off Ben's hot forehead.

"Oh, I don't know," Rachel said. "Maybe it prepares them for life. My mother died when I wasn't much older than Ben, and I survived pretty well, don't you think?"

When John didn't answer, Rachel jokingly jabbed his arm. "What's the matter? Don't you think I turned out okay?"

John obviously wasn't in the mood for teasing. He turned to face Rachel and looked straight into her eyes. "Rachel, you're 62 years old and, from what you've told me, you've fallen in love for the first time. And now I get the distinct impression that you're having second thoughts about marrying me. Yes, Rachel, you've survived, but I want more than survival for Ben. I want him to live a full life, free from fear that he's going to die. Or, worse yet, lose the ones he loves. I want more for him, Rachel. Much more."

John rose from his chair and started to leave the room. Hand on the door, he stopped and turned back. "Want anything from the cafeteria?"

Rachel, speechless, shook her head. She didn't know what to say. As if on cue, the door opened, and Stan Berninger poked his head in.

"My god, Rachel, what's going on here? You all look worse than little Lily, and she's been bitten by a pit bull dog."

"Hey, Stan," Rachel said. "You know John, don't you?"

The two men shook hands, and Stan walked over to the bed, lowering his voice so as not to wake Ben.

"How are they treating the little fellow? Sorry I haven't gotten over here sooner. Been out of town. Got the call about Lily yesterday and came on back."

"How is she?"

"Well, lucky the dog got her where he did. On her upper thigh and not somewhere the scars will show. She'll heal. At least on the outside. Her mama said the nightmares last night were pretty bad."

Rachel remembered the times Lily had been to her office with

Stan and how much she loved playing with Ralph. Such a trusting child. So affectionate. Images of her blond curls buried in his thick black fur flooded into Rachel's mind. She didn't want to ask Stan how the attack had happened, but he offered the details in the way he always told Lily stories. As if everyone would want to know all about anything that had to do with his granddaughter.

"She was over at a friend's house, playing, and the family got a new dog," Stan explained. "Had him about a month. No problems. Seemed to get along well with the children and other dogs. The whole kit and kaboodle. Kids were outside playing tag. And when Lily ran over to tag the kid, the dog lunged for her. Mother heard her screaming and ran out and pulled him off."

"Stan, I'm so sorry. Anything I can do to help, you let me know."

"Dog's been put down. Nothing more to do, I guess. Parents aren't the type to press charges. Just glad he didn't get her face." Stan rubbed his hand across his eyes and reached in his back pocket for a handkerchief. He blew his nose noisily.

Ben stirred in the bed across the room and opened his eyes. "Granddaddy? Where's Rachel? Ralph? Where's Ralph? I need Ralph," the boy wailed.

Oh, no, not this again, Rachel thought. I had hoped we'd gotten beyond that little scenario. But no, Ben continued to cry for the dog until a nurse rushed in and gave him another shot.

"You really must try to keep him quiet," the nurse blustered. "The only way we can keep the fever down is to keep him from being upset. There are too many people in the room. One of you needs to leave," she said, looking pointedly at Stan.

"On my way out now, lady," he said. "Stop by and see Lily when you can, Rachel. She could use some cheering up."

Rachel said she'd be down a little later and hugged Stan good-bye. The nurse followed him and firmly closed the door behind her.

"I guess they're feeling a little overprotective after the episode with Belle and Mary," John muttered in defense of the overbearing nurse.

"No need to be rude though," Rachel said. By then, Ben had settled back to sleep. "Still going to the cafeteria?"

John nodded, jingling the coins in his pocket.

"See if they've got any jasmine tea," Rachel said. "I could sure use a cup."

* * *

When Rachel checked her cellphone messages later, she found one from Carrie. Short and to the point, the young woman said she'd turned in her notice at work and wanted to talk to Rachel about taking over the reins at The Gilbert Companies.

Well, that didn't take long, Rachel thought. Wonder how Horace Junior feels about this. As much as she wished her own life were simpler, she'd still rather have her challenges than the ones Carrie faced. John's jealousy over George had been short-lived compared to what Carrie faced if she suddenly became her future husband's boss.

And all the fear Rachel felt about the day-to-day life of a wife and mother at her age paled compared to what she imagined was in store for Carrie. If Horace Junior had inherited any of his father's stubbornness and ambition, the young woman would have a fight on her hands.

Always puts things into perspective, Rachel told herself, when you look outside yourself.

She made a note to return Carrie's call first thing the next morning. She wasn't sure whether to offer some unsolicited personal advice in addition to her legal services in documenting Carrie's position in the company. She realized she had absolutely no experience on which to base any advice in relationships. Still, she'd done a lot of observing in her 62 years, and many of her observations had been made as a divorce lawyer.

She looked across the room at John, napping in the recliner. She sipped her tea, cool now after sitting on the ledge beside her chair for several hours. The hospital lay quiet around her. Nobody bustled up and down the halls. At least for the moment. No announcement had blared over the loudspeaker in a while. Rachel had turned off the lights and sat in the dark, breathing, trying to calm her monkey mind. She hoped she could nap for awhile. Her body was tired after a busy day, but her mind just wouldn't let go of its work.

She remembered what her grandmother had taught her to do when she had trouble sleeping as a child. "Hold yourself like a baby and rock back and forth," she had said. For years, Rachel had forgotten the advice that had worked so well for the little girl who had lost her mother's arms. She didn't know what had prompted the memory now, so many years later as she sat in a big city hospital room. But she grabbed on to her arms with the opposite hands and began to rock. Within minutes, her eyes grew heavy and she felt herself falling into that delicious place of unconsciousness.

Chapter Eighteen

When Rachel opened her cellphone to return Carrie's phone call the next day, a message from Susan waited to be retrieved from her voicemail box.

"Okay, Rachel," her friend began. "Today's the day you have GOT to make a decision about the wedding. To postpone or not to postpone, that is the question. Call me. We've got to let the florist know. We've got to call the caterer. We need to . . ." Susan was mercifully cut off before she could finish her list of things that needed to be done.

Rachel sighed. She took three deep breaths and hit the speed dial button. Susan answered on the third ring, sounding breathless.

"You okay?" Rachel asked. "You sound out of breath."

"Dancing," Susan said.

Rachel heard Aretha Franklin in the background, singing "Chain of Fools".

"Wait a minute. Let me turn the music off so I can hear you."

Rachel heard Susan's tap shoes patter across the linoleum of her kitchen floor and then a moment of silence before she tapped her way back to the wall phone. She breathed a long sigh, and Rachel pictured her sitting at the kitchen table with today's to-do list in front of her.

"How's Ben?" Susan asked.

Rachel told her about the recent setback and the restless night she and John suffered as nurses bustled in and out to check on him.

"He was still asleep when I left a little while ago. It's not good,

Susan. I'm worried about John as much as Ben. He's taking this very hard."

"Maybe I should take Ralph back," Susan said. "It seemed to work before."

"No, Susan, you don't need to take Ralph back. Ben needs to stay quiet. They say he had too much excitement, and they're trying to make sure he doesn't get overstimulated."

Rachel listened to the silence and knew that Susan felt disappointment at being told to stay away, but, after she agreed to wait at least 24 hours before her next visit, Susan launched into another course of action.

"I know you don't want to talk about this, Rachel, but as your best friend and wedding planner, I must tell you that today is the day . . ."

"I know. I know," Rachel interrupted. "Go ahead and postpone things. In fact, let's move it forward a couple of months."

"Do you need to talk to John about this? Does he know?"

"No, he doesn't know, but I'm sure he'll agree. No way Ben will be well enough for us to leave him and go away in a month."

"Yes, you really MUST have a honeymoon."

"So, go ahead and stop the presses."

"Well, don't say 'stop,' Rachel. We're just slowing them down a little, right?"

"Right," Rachel said. "Gotta go, now. Georgia's got some papers for me to sign at the office. Then I need to get back to the hospital." Rachel prepared to end the conversation and then remembered she hadn't said one thing of the utmost importance. "Thanks, Susan. You've given me quite a gift. Something I couldn't give myself."

"What's that, honey?"

"Permission to do this. I'm so relieved you made me take some action today. I was getting so tired of thinking about what to do. Thanks."

"Okay. Just make sure you're . . ."

"Gotta go. Love ya."

Rachel hung up before Susan could start on a lecture about how wonderful John was and how wonderful marriage was and how she shouldn't use Ben's hospitalization as an excuse for not going through with the wedding at all. Susan knows me too well, Rachel thought.

"Come on, Ralph," she called to the dog. "We need a trip to the Circle."

Ralph ran to the spot where his leash hung and grabbed it in his mouth.

"You have no trouble making decisions, do you, sir? Ah, to be a dog."

Rachel felt herself unwinding with each step she took toward Dupont Circle. Each time Ralph stopped to sniff at his favorite places – a fire hydrant, a telephone pole, a neighbor's fence – she stood still and breathed. Each time she stood, she felt the tension leave her shoulders, the place she had carried stress for a lifetime.

And with the brisk walk in between each pause, she focused on moving forward, away from her obsessive thinking. Thinking about how to tell John she had postponed the wedding without discussing it with him. Thinking about Ben and whether he was receiving the right treatment. Trust came hard for Rachel, and she was very aware that she had no control over Ben's health. Thinking about Belle and whether she had told Ricky that George was coming. Thinking about Carrie and whether she was about to make a huge mistake, jeopardizing her relationship by taking control of the company.

"Damn you, Horace. You're still causing complications even from the grave," she muttered.

Ralph pulled on the leash, bringing her back to the moment. The walk. "Be here now," he seemed to say, and Rachel smiled. Thanks, pal. What would I do without you in my life?

A young mother pushed a stroller toward them, and Rachel stopped walking so the toddler could pet Ralph. "How wonderful that she's not afraid of him," Rachel said.

"Yeah. She's only a little more than a year old. Hasn't learned to be afraid yet."

"Let's hope she stays that way."

"She won't," the woman said, "but maybe she can hold on to it for a little while longer."

Ralph shot out his long wet tongue and gave the child a huge slobbery lick on the face. She wrinkled up her nose, shut her eyes tight and squealed with delight. Ralph tugged on his leash as if to say, "There are other people who need my love. Let's go."

Belle and Mary walked toward them as Rachel and Ralph turned the corner on to O Street. Mary had reached the age when she felt much too old to ride in a stroller. Her insistence that she walk beside her mother made their trips to the Circle a long, slow journey. Rachel smiled as she observed Belle's patience with her daughter's small steps and her frequent stops to look at things along the way. A bottle cap, a candy wrapper or a shiny piece of glass all deserved her full attention.

We can learn so much from children, Rachel thought and said a silent "thank you" for the fact that she had two small children in her world after a lifetime of none.

As she drew closer to the pair, she saw a look of concern on Belle's face and suspected it had something to do with George's upcoming visit.

"Morning," she called out. "Where are you two going?"

"Off to meet Ricky," Belle said. "He's taking Mary without me for the first time, and I'm a little nervous."

"I'm sure they'll be fine. Deejee will be with them, right?"

"Yes. They're going to the zoo."

"Have you told him about George coming yet?"

Even before Belle said "no," Rachel knew. The girl's downcast eyes gave away the answer. Before Rachel could protest, Belle launched into a defense.

"I'm going to tell him today when he brings Mary home. I didn't want to ruin their time together. I'm not sure how Ricky's going to react, and if he gets in a foul mood, I don't want Mary to be with him. Sorry if you think I've done the wrong thing, Rachel. I'm doing the best I can."

Belle picked Mary up and stormed off before Rachel had a chance to say anything. Not good, Rachel muttered to herself. Not good, Ralph. People make life so complicated for themselves, don't they? As if in answer, Ralph lifted his leg and relieved himself on Susan's azalea bushes.

Once inside, Rachel took a few minutes to check messages and grab a quick bite to eat before she headed back to the hospital. She retrieved a phone message from her cousin Nancy in Virginia, asking if she needed any help with the wedding. "I keep thinking how lovely you're going to look in your grandmother's dress," she said. "She'd be so happy to know you found it, just in time. See you soon."

Oh, dear. I've got to get in touch with the people who've been invited, Rachel thought.

"Like I said, Ralph, people sure do complicate life."

Rachel ran upstairs and washed her face, trying to get the city grit off. She looked at her reflection in the mirror and took a deep breath. The eyes that stared back at her looked like they belonged to a scared rabbit.

"Who are you?" she asked the mirror.

When no answer came, she sat down on the tub, continuing to hold the cool, wet washcloth. She swiped at the back of her neck a couple of times and listened to the drip of the faucet. Finally, she stood up and tightened the cold and hot water handles and hung the washcloth back on the rack.

Leigh Somerville

"Ralph, you and I haven't been to our meditation room in more than a week, and it's beginning to show. Come on. Time's a wasting."

The dog ran ahead of her and up two flights of stairs. He sat on the window seat with his tongue hanging out, panting, when Rachel walked in the door, as if to say, "What took you so long?"

Rachel sat down on her zafu and took several deep breaths. She closed her eyes and began to focus inward. Within a few breaths, she felt her shoulder muscles relax. Her hands loosened from the fists she realized she had clenched. Her jaw grew slack, and her heart rate began to slow.

When the phone rang, Rachel ignored the sound and returned to focusing on her breath. Soon, Ralph began to snore, and she smiled at the comforting sound.

Chapter Nineteen

John stood at the nurse's station, chatting with Ben's doctor when Rachel stepped out of the elevator. The smiles on their faces relieved Rachel's anxiety. Surely, Ben must be doing better, she thought.

"Good evening," Dr. Cox said as she drew nearer. "You'll be happy to hear that Mr. Ben's temperature has gone back down already. I think we've got his condition stabilized again. But, please, no more parties in his room. Let's keep him quiet, at least until he gets home, okay?"

John and Rachel promised they'd restrict visitors and try to keep the boy on a low simmer for the rest of his hospital stay.

"I understand he had a visit from a seeing-eye dog," Dr. Cox said, waiting for an explanation. When none came, she smiled. "I know how much he wanted to see his own dog. So glad a substitute meant so much to him."

"Yes, the visit really seemed to help," Rachel said. "Maybe the hospital should reconsider its policy on pets in the rooms."

"Maybe," Dr. Cox said, looking none too sure. "Well, I need to get on with my rounds. The staff has my orders for the night. I'll be back tomorrow morning to check on him. Hopefully, he's turned the corner again and will be going home by the end of next week."

After the doctor left, John pulled Rachel into an embrace that felt more like it came from a drowning man than a lover. Rachel pulled back a little from the sensation of clinging, of being pulled under with him.

"What's wrong?" he asked, sensing her resistance. "Everything okay at home?"

Rachel nodded and started to walk into Ben's room.

"Great news about the possibility of Ben going home next week," he said. "That means we can move forward with the wedding plans next month."

"John, I've already told Susan to stop everything. The photographer. The caterer. They all needed to know something yesterday."

John grabbed Rachel's arm and jerked her around to face him. His eyes looked like a huge, black thundercloud. "You did this without talking to me?"

"Well, yes, John. I figured you had enough on your mind with Ben. I really didn't think we had any choice. There didn't seem to be anything to talk about."

John stood still, towering over her, rigid, cold, no longer touching her. He folded his arms across his chest. His mouth tensed in a grim line. "Really. I thought a wedding was a joint venture, not a solo practice, Rachel. Obviously, you don't agree."

Rachel stepped back, out of the range of John's anger, shocked by the intensity of his reaction. She wasn't entirely surprised by his words, but the passion with which he spoke them caught her off-guard. From her years of experience practicing law, she went into defense mode.

"John, you're overacting. We're just postponing the ceremony a little. No big deal." She made a move toward the door. Again, John pulled her back.

"Maybe to you, Rachel. You're the one in control. I don't like this feeling. I don't like it at all." He glared at her, and his grip on her arm tightened.

"John, let go of my arm. You're hurting me. I'm going in to see Ben now. We'll talk about this later. When you've calmed down."

"Maybe," he said. "Maybe we'll talk about it, and maybe we won't." He stormed off toward the elevator.

Right before the door closed behind him, Rachel saw him pull his cellphone out of his pocket. She wondered whose number he punched in so furiously.

Inside the room, Ben's eyes lay closed, and his chest rose and fell in sleep. Light from the bathroom shone across the bed, leaving the rest of the room in dim shadows. Rachel sat down heavily in the recliner beside his bed and matched her breathing to his.

"Oh, Ben, what have I gotten myself into?" she whispered.

So many times in the months since John and Ben had left her downstairs apartment and moved upstairs into Rachel's house, she had questioned her decision to get involved. Even in the smoothest of times, she feared complications that might hurt Ben. It was bad enough when two adults made wrong judgment calls and got hurt, but Rachel had seen too many situations at work where innocent children had been pulled through all the turmoil of a messy divorce. Now, as she looked at Ben, sleeping the sleep of the blissfully unaware, she was afraid that he would be the one to suffer most now.

A tap on the door interrupted her thoughts, and she looked up to see Susan, standing in the door holding a present covered with multicolored ribbons. Rachel held her fingers to her lips. Susan tiptoed in the room, laid the gift at the bottom of the bed and sat in the extra chair.

"What's wrong with you?" she said. "You look like you've lost your best friend."

"I may have. John's furious about my postponing the wedding without talking to him."

"Rachel, I warned you about that."

"I don't need any 'I told you so's.' The man's a control freak. Better to find out now than after we get married."

"Now, Rachel, don't go all to pieces. Just ride it out. These little things always work out. Look at Jim and me. We've been through a major challenge, and it's just brought us closer. You and John will be fine. Give him a few days to get over his hurt feelings and then talk to him about setting a new date. Emphasis on 'talk to him.' Hear me?"

Rachel sat, stony-faced and silent. Her eyes, when she finally turned them toward her friend, didn't hold much promise.

"Oh, dear, I've seen that look before," Susan said. "Lord, help us all."

* * *

When she woke up at three a.m., Rachel was surprised to realize that John had not returned to the hospital. She asked the nurse checking Ben's temperature if she had seen him during the night.

"No. He called at about ten o'clock and said he was going to stay at home and try to get some rest. He asked us to call him if there were any change. And he asked if you were still here."

"Oh, really?"

Rachel didn't understand how John, who had been so reluctant to go down to the cafeteria for a cup of coffee even, had been able to leave the hospital completely. Another red flag, she thought. If he can abandon his grandson like this just because he's mad at me, he's not the man I thought he was.

Rachel walked into the bathroom, ran cold water into a paper cup and drank deeply. When she looked into the mirror, she paused at what she saw. The woman looking back at her seemed to have aged ten years in a matter of hours. All the light had left her eyes, and the frown lines had reappeared between them. She turned out the bathroom light and fumbled back to the recliner in the dark.

* * *

John walked into Ben's room behind the orderly who carried the breakfast tray. He avoided Rachel's eyes and moved to Ben's side.

"Morning, Tiger. How are you feeling this morning?"

Still sleepy, Ben mumbled something and then sat up straighter when he saw the present Susan had left the night before. "Wow. Is that for me, Rachel?"

"Yes, Susan came to see you last night while you were sleeping and left it. Why don't you eat your breakfast first so it won't get cold, and then you can see what's in it."

Ben poked his bottom lip out and crossed his little arms across his chest. Where have I seen that look before, Rachel asked herself.

"I can take over now, Rachel," John said. "Why don't you go on and leave. Thanks for staying last night."

Stunned at being so coolly dismissed like a hired hand, Rachel gathered her jacket and purse and stood slowly. As she turned toward the door, John handed Ben the present, and the child tore at the ribbons in great glee.

Rachel closed the door behind her and walked slowly down the hall.

* * *

Rachel didn't even stop to check her phone messages when she returned home. Instead, she headed to her third floor meditation room, with Ralph trailing behind her. She took time to light a stick of sandalwood incense and several candles and put Leonard Cohen on the CD player. As she settled on her zafu, she saw Ralph staring at her from the window seat. Like an embrace, they held each other's gaze for a few long minutes. Rachel took three deep breaths and felt her body begin to relax as the tense muscles up and down her back let go.

She focused on her breath and tried to release the obsessive thoughts of John. Off and on, her mind wrestled with the image of his glare, and each time she refocused on the simple act of breathing. After about five minutes, she was tempted to give up. This isn't working, she thought. I might as well go downstairs and pay bills. Maybe I should call Susan and ask if she wants to go to the Eastern Market.

But each time the thought of giving up rose, she told herself she'd sit for five more minutes. The phone rang a couple of times, and she ignored it. Finally, after the third ring, she gave up, blew out the candles and turned off Leonard.

Ralph looked at her as if to say, "You woos."

"Hey, I sat for 30 minutes, pal. Give me a break."

Ralph laid his head back down on his paws and closed his eyes. Rachel recovered the three messages from her answering machine. One from Belle, in tears. One from Mrs. Moser next door, checking on Ben, and the final message from Susan, asking her if she wanted to go to the Eastern Market.

"Great minds run along the same track," Rachel said when Susan answered the phone.

"Does that mean you want to go?"

"Yes, as long as you can give me a few minutes to get ready. And I need to call Belle, too. Something's evidently going on downstairs. She left a message, and she sounded like she was crying."

"Yeah, I saw Ricky storm out of her apartment the other day when he brought Mary home. What's going on? I thought they were getting along so well."

"Not sure. Let me give her a ring. What time do you want to leave?"

"Think you can be ready in half an hour?"

Rachel assured her friend she could and hung up. Belle answered the phone almost before it had a chance to ring and went into the tearful story of Ricky's reaction to the news of George's visit.

"Well, surely you're not surprised," Rachel said and then wished she had been more tactful. Belle burst into more tears. "Do you want to come up and talk about it? I'm leaving in about 30 minutes, but we can talk while I'm getting ready."

Belle hesitated, but Rachel knew the pause meant she needed help.

"Tell you what, the kitchen door's unlocked. I'll be upstairs dressing. Come on in if you want to."

As Rachel walked upstairs to brush her teeth and rebraid her hair, she thought about Belle downstairs, crying with the frustration of being caught between her former life and the promise of one so different. What in the world do I have to offer her, she wondered. I've got my own dilemma.

But when she looked up and saw the young woman's tear-stained face, she knew the answer and took mother and child in her arms. Mary wiped tears from Belle's cheeks.

"Mommy's sad," she told Rachel. "Daddy yelled at us."

"Daddy didn't yell at you, Mary. Just me."

"No, Daddy yelled at me, too," the little girl insisted. "Daddy's mad."

"Mary, why don't you sit over here and brush Ralph while Mommy and I talk," Rachel said, handing the child a wire brush.

Ralph looked up with his tongue hanging out in a smile. Belle nodded to Mary, giving her permission.

"Thanks, Rachel," she said.

"Here, sit down in the rocker while I get dressed. Is it still cool enough for a jacket?"

Belle nodded as Rachel stepped into the closet and chose a beige linen jacket and black tee shirt to wear with her jeans.

"I take it Ricky wasn't very happy about the news that George is coming tomorrow?"

"He threatened me."

Rachel dropped the jacket. She stooped over to pick it up, giving herself time to collect her thoughts. "What do you mean he 'threatened' you?"

"He said if I got involved with another man, I'd be sorry."

"Well, what do you think he meant by that?"

"I don't know. He wouldn't talk to me. He just left, and I haven't heard from him since."

"So, is he going to watch Mary while George is here?"

"I don't know. He didn't stay long enough to make plans. And I don't know now if I want her with him while he's so angry. I'm afraid of what he might do."

Rachel agreed that she should make other plans for a babysitter and offered to do what she could to help.

"In fact, John seems to need me less often at the hospital, so I should be around more. Relax, Belle, all is well. Try to let this thing with Ricky go. He's acting like a spoiled child. Hopefully, he'll shift back into his role as an adult soon, and everything will work out."

Rachel snapped the beads onto the end of her braid and slipped on her Birkenstocks. "In fact, why don't you let me watch her tomorrow night so you can go ahead and make plans."

"Thanks, Rachel. I guess I can do that. Where are you off to?"

"An adventure with Susan. It's been too long. I need a Susan fix to cure what ails me."

Chapter Twenty

Rachel laughed at the contrast between her own jeans, black tee shirt and beige linen jacket and Susan's hot pink jogging suit.

"Good to see you laughing, but what's so funny?" Susan asked as she opened her front door.

"Look at us. We're such opposites. Do you ever wonder what we're doing together?"

"It's simple. We love each other." Susan bounded off the bottom step and rushed down the sidewalk. She stopped at the corner and waited for Rachel to catch up with her.

"What in the world are you carrying in that huge satchel?" she asked.

Rachel had slung a tiny bag across her shoulder, big enough for her house key, lipstick and some money. In contrast, Susan looked like she had planned an overnight stay. Her straw bag bulged with stuff that threatened to spill out and leave a trail behind them.

"Rachel, you never know what you may need when you leave the comforts of home. I like to be prepared, so I brought a few things with me. Don't you worry."

Susan pulled Rachel across the street with her and finally down the steps to the metro station. When they reached the machine that dispensed subway tickets, Rachel laughed when Susan didn't have money to buy one.

"What's wrong with you?" Rachel asked. "You seem to have everything but the kitchen sink in there and yet you forgot money."

"Rachel Springer, I've got a lot on my mind, if you must know."

The train roared into the station, drowning out Susan's words. The two crowded onto the first available car and found a seat near the back. Susan sat buried beneath her huge bag, taking up more than her half of the seat.

"So, what's going on?" Rachel finally asked.

"Well, I guess this is as good a time as any to tell you, although Jim doesn't want the word to get out yet so you need to keep it to yourself, okay?"

Rachel assured her friend she wouldn't tell a soul and waited for Susan's dramatic pause to end.

"Jim wants to retire."

Rachel grabbed her friend in the best bear hug she could manage with an obstacle between the two. Susan had expressed a desire for Jim's retirement for years, hoping they could spend more time together and with their family.

Pulling back, Rachel realized her friend wasn't hugging her back. "So, why the long face? This is what you've been wanting for years, isn't it?"

"There's more."

"Okay."

"He wants to sell our house and move to the beach. To Pawley's Island. South Carolina."

Rachel's mouth dropped open.

"He wants to go fishing every day." Susan stared straight ahead, but Rachel could see enough of her friend's face, even from the side, to know that she was none too pleased about her husband's plans.

"My god, Susan. How long have you all been talking about this? When does he want to stop work? When does he want to move?"

Susan shook her head and hunkered further over the straw bag as if to achieve some kind of support from its contents. "We've fantasized about it for years. About retiring to the beach. But now that the time has come, the reality feels different than the dream. And I guess my idea evolved more into a weekend place somewhere close to DC so we could keep the house here."

The train ground to a halt at the Eastern Market station, and Rachel helped Susan stand. The two merged into the mass of people leaving the car and moved with the flow up the escalator and into the daylight.

Rachel loved the rush of color that always hit her with a carnival atmosphere. The smell of funnel cakes and Turkish coffee. The cacophony of voices cackling in several different languages.

But this morning, the effect seemed dulled by the shock of Susan's news. Rachel guided her friend to a bench where they sat in silence for a few minutes.

"When does he want to do this?" she asked again.

"He's ready to retire immediately. In fact, he's planning to give his letter of resignation Monday, with a month's notice. He wants to start interviewing realtors this weekend."

Rachel couldn't imagine life without Susan across the street. When she looked at her friend, she remembered all they had shared. Susan averted her eyes.

"Has he asked for your opinion, or is he going ahead with plans without you?"

Susan nodded. "We've talked. I just don't know, Rachel. I want it all. I want to move to the beach, but I don't want to leave." At that, Susan burst into tears.

Rachel rummaged around in the straw bag for Kleenex. She found a bottle opener, a mini cutting board, moist wipes, but no Kleenex. She walked over to the funnel cake cart and asked for a napkin. Returning to the bench, she handed it to Susan and sat back down with her.

"Susan, I don't know what to say. This is such a surprise to me. Guess I had no idea you all were even thinking about doing something like this. It'll take a few days for it to sink in."

Suddenly, the air was pierced by a loud squeal. "Mommy, look!" a child screamed. "It's her. It's the poem lady."

Rachel looked up to see a large black woman being pulled toward them by a little girl with a huge grin on her face. The woman looked embarrassed. "Sorry," she said. "Sorry to interrupt. She's been looking for you every Saturday since you wrote that poem for her. She loves it so much that she sleeps with it."

"See, Mommy. I told you she'd come back." The little girl approached Susan and laid a little hand on her knee, tapping it tentatively. "Write me another poem, poem lady. I want to give one to my friend."

Susan's face broke into a smile as she poked through her bag and pulled out a pencil and notebook.

"See, Rachel. Got to be prepared." Turning to the child, she asked what kind of poem she wanted.

"A good-bye poem. My best friend is moving away, and I need a magic poem so I won't lose her."

Susan looked at Rachel and smiled. And as she began to write, Rachel remembered something her friend had told her the first day she had set up her lawn chair and the sign advertising "poetry on demand."

"Art heals," Susan had said when Rachel asked why she was doing it. And, now, as she watched the joy spread across Susan's face as she wrote, she understood the truth in those words.

Five minutes ago, her friend had sunk into blackness. Now, as she scratched words across the page, she radiated light. The little girl stared up at her as if she were looking at an angel.

Rachel stood up and slung her purse over her shoulder. "I'll leave you two to your magic," she said. "I'm going for a walk. Be back in a few minutes. Susan, can I bring you something? Coffee?"

"No, I'm fine."

"So I see," Rachel said and patted her friend's shoulder as she walked away.

The morning air felt hotter than usual, and, within a few minutes, sweat ran down Rachel's back. She picked up a flyer lying on the ground and began to fan herself with it.

"Hot enough for you?" she heard a young man ask. She turned to see him sitting in a wheelchair. A baseball cap covered most of his face. He tilted it back on his head so he could get a better look at her.

"Oh, sorry," he said. "I thought you were someone else. Someone I know. A neighbor."

Rachel smiled. "Not a problem. People do that to me all the time. Guess I've got a common face."

"Not at all. You have a very uncommon face, but you do have a twin," the young man said with a chuckle. "And she lives in the apartment next door to me." He stuck out his hand, and Rachel shook it. "Mike. Mike Alexander," he said.

"Nice to meet you, Mike. I'm Rachel Springer. Is that your guitar?" she asked, pointing to the case propped on the bench next to Mike's wheelchair.

He nodded and tipped the ball cap back over his eyes.

"You play?"

Another nod.

"Where do you play? I'm always looking for music, especially somebody new."

"You're looking at it," Mike said, sweeping his hands across the scene in front of them.

Then Rachel noticed the jar in his lap. Dollar bills and coins filled it almost to the top.

"Did I miss the show? I'd love to hear you play. I don't think I've . . ." Rachel stopped, embarrassed by what she had almost said.

"Never heard a gimpy rock star, right? Don't be embarrassed. It's probably why I get tipped so well. Folks feel sorry for me. Of course, some probably think it's a gimmick, like the blind guys in the subway. But trust me, I'm no gimmick." Mike slapped at his withered legs and pulled out a cigarette. "Got a light?"

"Sorry. Don't smoke. I could probably find you one though."

"No. That's okay. I'm on my way home. Got time for one last song though, if you'd like. Got a request?"

"What kind of music do you play?"

"What kind of music do you listen to?"

"Leonard Cohen?"

"Temple of Doom?"

Rachel smiled. Mike leaned over and opened his guitar case and pulled out an instrument that looked like it had traveled the world. When Mike began to pluck the strings, Rachel felt sure it had. Within a few chords, a crowd had gathered, and when she closed her eyes, she could have sworn she was sitting with Leonard.

Magic, she thought. The world is full of it.

"Rachel, you okay?"

She opened her eyes. Mike's playing had stopped, and they were alone again. The jar overflowed with more money.

"Yes, I'm fine. Better than fine. You're really good, you know. This is the only place you play?"

"Yes. It's perfect, don't you think? Low overhead. Nobody to cramp my style. Can't imagine any place I'd rather be. Play when I want to. No demands. Very few complaints. Life is good."

Rachel smiled. "Guess you're right. Thanks. Thanks for the fix."

"Sure thing." Mike started to wheel away and then stopped and turned back toward her. "By the way," he yelled back, "you're prettier than your twin."

Rachel waved and turned back to find Susan. The folding chair sat empty, but a sign was propped in it with a message that read, "Back Soon."

Rachel took a seat and sipped on the lemonade she had bought during her walk back to find her friend. A man's voice interrupted her thoughts. "Excuse me. I'd like to purchase a poem."

Rachel stared speechlessly and then remembered Susan's sign, "Poetry on Demand. $5 a Poem."

"Oh, I'm sorry. I'm not the one you're looking for."

"But your sign says you write poetry," the man insisted, growing red in the face. His voice rose in irritation.

"Yes, it does, but I didn't put the sign there. My friend did, and she's stepped away for a few minutes."

"But you're sitting there. You're sitting in the poetry chair. You're supposed to write poems."

Rachel looked at the man and wondered if he were crazy. He looked normal enough. Neatly cropped hair and beard, wire-rimmed glasses and a light blue broadcloth shirt and neatly pressed chinos.

"I'm very sorry, sir, but I'm sure you wouldn't be at all happy with any poem I wrote," Rachel assured him, standing to emphasize her point. "If you want to wait a minute, I'm sure Susan will be right back."

The man looked to the right, then to the left and finally huffed off in disgust. Just as he disappeared out of sight, Susan rounded the corner.

"You're not going to believe this," Rachel said. "I've got a story to tell you that takes poetry "on demand" to a whole new level."

Chapter Twenty-One

Later that day, Rachel headed to her back courtyard to enjoy the afternoon sun. She carried a glass of iced tea with her and eased down into one of the Adirondack chairs. Ralph dropped down in the shade at her feet.

The noise of Saturday traffic wasn't as loud as during the week, and Rachel pretended to sit in the yard on the farm. She breathed in deeply and let the air from her lungs out in a long sigh. What will I do if Susan really moves, she asked herself the second time she exhaled. I can't stand the idea of not being able to run across the street to visit on the spur of the moment.

She feasted on the memories of all the two friends had shared, and a hole seemed to have opened up inside her, threatening to suck her whole world into it.

Ralph sensed trouble and licked her hand. "Thanks, friend. You're the only one I have who understands."

"Now, wait a minute, How about me?"

Rachel looked up at John as he stood on the deck behind her. She jumped up, almost turning over her chair in the process. "John, what are you doing home? Why aren't you with Ben? What's going on?"

John walked down the steps into the courtyard and over to where Rachel stood. He stopped a few feet from her and waited to gauge her reaction before he moved any closer. Not sure, he stopped.

"Belle and Mary stopped by. I decided to take advantage of their visit to come home for a few minutes. I needed to see you, Rachel. To talk."

Rachel lowered her eyes and waited for him to go on. When he didn't, she sat back down in her chair and motioned for him to join her in the other.

"Can I get you something to drink?" she asked.

He shook his head and leaned it back against the wooden chair. As he looked up at the treetops, he considered how to begin. Rachel waited in silence.

Finally, he took a deep breath and reached out to take her hand. "Rachel, I'm sorry. I'm sorry for the way I overreacted to the change in wedding plans. I guess I got scared that you didn't want to marry me. Can you forgive me?"

Rachel squeezed his hand and nodded. "I'm sorry, too. That I didn't talk to you. I just thought . . ."

"I know. You thought I wouldn't want to be bothered. Can we start over? I don't want to lose you, Rachel. I need you in my life."

"I feel the same way. Especially now."

"Why? What's happened?"

"Susan told me today that she and Jim are planning to move. I can't believe it. I can't imagine some stranger living across the street. And Belle and Mary will probably move to the farm to be with George and . . ."

"Now, wait a minute," John laughed. "Aren't you doing just what I apologized for? Overreacting? George and Belle aren't even really dating yet, and you've got them moving in together."

Rachel smiled and rose to share John's. "Maybe so," she whispered in his ear. "How soon do you need to be back at the hospital?"

"Belle said to take my time, and I intend to do just that."

* * *

Rachel rode back to the hospital in the backseat of a cab with John, happy to sit close to him and hold hands like young lovers. She thought about how close she'd come to losing the gift that had become so important to her. She wondered how she had lived so long and so happily without a partner in her life. She realized how much richer her days had grown now that she shared them.

"When are Susan and Jim thinking about moving?" John asked, breaking the comfortable silence between them.

"I don't know. He's giving his notice Monday, and they're interviewing realtors this weekend. He's not the kind to let any grass grow under his feet once he's made a decision."

"What about Susan's decision?"

"She'll go along with whatever ride he wants to take."

"Not like you, right?"

Rachel glanced at John to gauge his mood. She wasn't sure how much teasing was behind the remark. In response, she reached up and pinched his nose. She was relieved they had arrived at the hospital, and that the conversation was cut short.

John paid the cab driver and took Rachel's hand in his again. "Thanks for coming back with me. It's so much easier having you here. I missed you."

"No, you didn't. You were too mad to miss me," Rachel laughed, jabbing him on the shoulder.

Belle greeted them with a smile as they walked in the room. "Good to see you guys looking so happy," she said. "Do I need to find another babysitter for Mary for tomorrow night?"

Rachel assured her that she looked forward to an evening with Mary. She planned to order a pizza and watch "The Little Mermaid". George was due to arrive around two o'clock in a smart effort to beat the rush hour traffic. Rachel had tidied up Ben's room so that he could stay there overnight. John had looked a little skeptical when she told him of the sleeping arrangements but had done a good job of restraining himself from saying anything. Rachel knew him well enough by now to be aware of his jealous streak. She admired his efforts to keep it in check.

"Any sign of the doctor while I was gone?" John asked Belle.

She told him that Dr. Cox had come by shortly after she arrived, and that her report had been good. "In fact, she said if he has a good weekend, she may let him go home by the end of next week."

"Yup. Tell Ralph I'm coming home," Ben squealed. John laid his hand on the boy's shoulder. "Not if you don't stay quiet. No squealing."

Ben frowned but did as he was told. Belle gathered up Mary and her toys and confirmed the plans for the next day. After the two left, the room grew quiet with the empty space that was left. Rachel noticed the frown on Ben's face had returned and asked him about it.

"I think I need to medidate," the child said.

"Meditate?" Rachel corrected him. "Why do you need to meditate, Ben?"

"I don't know. I just miss it. Can we meditate in the hospital?"

"Yes, especially in the hospital, Ben." She propped the pillows behind his back and showed him how to cross his legs. "John, you want to sit with us?"

And without hesitation, John Turner said he did. Rachel looked at Ben and winked as she turned out the overhead lights and sat back down in her chair. Within minutes, she heard a gentle snore from the man who was soon to be her husband, followed by a giggle from the boy in the bed.

* * *

Rachel returned to her office at the end of the day. Georgia watered the African violets on the front windowsill as she walked into the lobby.

"I don't know how you do it," Rachel said.

"Do what?"

"Keep all these things alive, along with all your other responsibilities."

"First of all, I name them instead of calling them 'things'," Georgia said. "Plants have feelings, too, you know."

Rachel walked over to the large fern sitting in the corner near her office door. "Sorry, Herbert," she muttered. "Didn't mean to hurt your feelings."

"Now you've really done it."

"What? What did I do now?"

"That's not Herbert. That's Sylvia. Maybe you'd better leave the talking to the plants to me." Georgia patted the fern and handed a file to her boss.

"Carrie's due here in about five minutes. Need anything other than her file?"

"Got any coffee?"

"Better start a fresh pot. That one's been sitting all day. When you're not here, it doesn't get drunk. How are things at the hospital?"

Rachel told her about Dr. Cox's hope that Ben might be able to return home in a week if he continued to improve. When she neared her desk, she noticed a pink phone message slip and picked it up. On it was scrawled the name "Ricky" and an exclamation point.

"What's this about?"

Georgia looked at Rachel and shook her head. "He called and left a message on the machine. Didn't leave a number, but said to tell you he'd taken Chelsea to an NA meeting. The rest was not fit to be repeated. He sounded drunk."

Rachel shook her head. "Isn't that just like life. He was able to help another suffering addict but couldn't help himself."

"What do you think set him off? I thought he was doing so well."

"I guess Belle told him about George coming."

"Is that restraining order still in effect?"

"Yes, but I don't know how much good it will do if he's drinking again."

The sound of the front door opening and closing interrupted the conversation. Georgia walked to the outer office to greet Carrie. As the young woman entered Rachel's office, she bit into a chocolate chip cookie. Rachel rose and moved around her desk to shake hands. She noticed lines had already begun to crease her client's forehead. Not a good sign, she thought. Maybe I should advise her to turn her back on Horace's company and return to her old job.

Instead, she opened the file and pretended to put papers in order to buy herself some time. Finally, she decided to stop ignoring the fact that the emperor wore no clothes. "Carrie, you look troubled. What's wrong?"

Carrie looked down at her hands and rubbed the finger where the missing diamond had sat. When she looked up, Rachel saw the tears in her eyes. "Horace Junior and I have broken up. Called off the wedding. He's talking about looking for a job and moving out of town."

Rachel stood up and walked around to the other side of her desk. She placed her hand on Carrie's shoulder and passed her a tissue from the box she kept within reach. "Carrie, I'm so sorry. What happened?"

Rachel felt she probably knew the answer without asking. Horace's son was even more egotistical than his father, if that were possible. Having his future wife at the helm of the family business, acting as HIS boss, was more than he could stomach. Rachel knew the best action she could take was to give her client the opportunity to tell the story. To get it off her chest.

"We ate dinner last night at the Brickskeller. We needed to go over a few final details about the wedding. Check the guest list one last time to make sure nobody had been left off before I ordered the invitations. I thought Horace might actually want to postpone the whole thing for a while, in consideration of his father's death and all, but Horace seems to be handling it pretty well and insisted we go on as planned."

Carrie started to cry again. Rachel poured a glass of water and passed it to her.

The young woman took a sip and forged on. "Everything was going so well. I guess I should have known, but I didn't. Or I didn't want to know."

Rachel nodded.

"When I told him I'd decided to quit my job and run The Gilbert Companies, he went ballistic. Didn't even give me a chance. Jumped up from the table before dinner was even served and stormed off."

"Have you talked to him since?"

"He won't return my phone calls. I got an email from him this morning telling me he was planning to leave the company and look for work in California."

"Can't get much further away than that, can you? Carrie, are you sure you want to do this? Is it worth it?"

Carrie set her jaw, and her eyes steeled with determination. Rachel saw sitting across the desk from her the reason Horace had made the decision to leave his company to this young woman. Carrie straightened her spine and threw her shoulders back.

"Where do I sign?"

* * *

Georgia's eyes focused on the pile of wadded up wet tissues as soon as she walked into Rachel's office. "Looks like you had an emotional meeting," she said. "What in the world happened?"

"Another man with a fragile ego. Another relationship bites the dust. Do you realize how lucky you are to have Will?"

"Every day of my life," Georgia said as she removed Carrie's file from the desk. "How about you? Are you and John back in the saddle?"

"Yes. In fact, we discussed honeymoon plans right before I left him. Although he said he wants the final destination to be a surprise for me."

"How romantic. What will you do about Ben?"

"We're thinking about taking him with us."

Georgia looked at the woman sitting in front of her and smirked.

"What?" Rachel asked. "He's part of this deal, too, you know. And this whole hospital scare has really shaken John. I don't think I could ask him to leave the boy behind so soon after we thought we were going to lose him."

"You're a good woman, Rachel Springer. You never cease to amaze me. You've waited all your life for a honeymoon, and now you're willing to share it with a child."

"Well, it's not exactly like I've sat around waiting 'all my life,' Georgia. I haven't made getting married a high priority, have I? This is not a big deal. We're all just going away for a little vacation."

"And Ralph? Is he going, too?"

"No, Belle will take care of Ralph."

"Speaking of Belle, has George arrived yet?"

"Should be there when I get home. I'm looking forward to seeing him. I think John will enjoy him now that he knows he's not a threat."

"Well, have fun. I'm going to make copies of these papers and get them in the mail to Carrie and then I'm leaving for the day. Will's got a follow-up appointment with his oncologist, and I want to go with him."

"See you tomorrow."

"Not likely. Tomorrow's Saturday."

Chapter Twenty-Two

A s Rachel turned the corner, she saw George had unloaded his pickup truck. She smiled at the sight of the beat-up red Chevy Silverado parked in front of her brownstone. It looked like a smile on the face of the tree-lined street of stately old buildings. A slightly snaggle-toothed smile, but a smile, nonetheless.

George looked up, caught sight of Rachel and waved. She picked up her pace, and he loped the rest of the distance to meet her.

"How was your trip?" Rachel asked in mid-hug. "Have any trouble finding us?"

"Let's just say I got a good look at the Washington Monument as I drove around and around it. Woman, you're even crazier than I thought you were, living in a place like this. I need to get Belle and Mary out of here, and the sooner the better."

"But look how lucky you are," Rachel said, pointing to the truck. "A parking space right at my front door." She leaned over and picked up a paper bag, loaded with corn. "Come on in, and I'll show you to your room. Belle and Mary must have walked to the Circle. I'm sure they'll be right back and delighted to see you. In the meantime, you'll just have to be satisfied with Ralph and me."

"And me," Susan chirped, rushing across the street. "You must be George," she gushed. "I've heard so much about you. First, from Rachel and now from Belle. My, aren't you just the bee's knees," Susan said, raring back and looking George up and down.

"George, this is my friend, Susan. Susan, this is George." George bowed and took Susan's hand and kissed it.

"Pleased to meet you, madam."

Susan followed Rachel and George up the sidewalk to the house where they heard Ralph bark with excitement on the other side of the door. When Rachel opened it, the dog bounded out to greet George like a long lost friend.

"Hey, boy. There's room in the truck for you, too. The city's no place for a dog. Imagine being penned up inside like this all day when just a few hours down the road you've got open fields and cows to play with."

"Now, wait a minute," Rachel said. "Don't you go trying to steal my dog, too."

Ralph ran circles around the group in the foyer and then dashed up the steps in front of Rachel, playing the role of host. Rachel showed George Ben's room and the bathroom down the hall. "Why don't you get settled in while I go downstairs and see about getting supper started. We'll eat at seven. That will give John time to make sure Ben has eaten before he has to leave the hospital."

"How is Ben?"

"Getting stronger every day. Children are amazing the way they can bounce back so quickly."

George nodded his head and walked over to the window and looked out at the street. He scratched his head and looked first one way and then the other. "What is it about this place you love, Rachel? I just don't see it."

Rachel smiled and shook her head. "If you have to ask, George, you'll never understand the answer. See you at dinner. I'll be on the lookout for Belle and let her know you're here as soon as she arrives."

"Thanks, but I don't see how she could possibly miss my truck unless she's gone blind since I last saw her."

Rachel laughed and started for the door. "Come on, Ralph. Time to eat."

The dog sat next to George and refused to budge.

"He's fine with me. Let him stay. I could use the company here in the big city."

Ralph wagged his tail, leaned against George for a few minutes and jumped up on the bed to seal the deal.

* * *

Susan sat at the kitchen table, sipping iced tea. "What a nice-looking man," she said, even before Rachel entered the room. "I like him."

"You don't even know him yet, but, yes, he is very likeable."

Rachel busied herself with preparations for dinner. She pulled plates out of the china cabinet, began to set the table and then turned to ask Susan if she'd like to join the group later to eat.

"No, Jim and I are having dinner with the realtor we think we're going to list the house with. Amy Justice. Do you know her?"

"I think I've heard the name. Pretty high-powered businesswoman, if I'm thinking of the right person."

"Jim says he's heard she's one of the best," Susan said as she took a long sip of tea and wiped her lips on the back of her hand.

Rachel handed her a napkin, which she twisted absentmindedly as she stared out the window at the courtyard. Rachel stood at the counter, shucked corn and waited for her friend to say more.

"The children aren't very happy about this," Susan finally said. "I mean, they're excited about us buying a place at the beach, but they don't want us to sell the house where they grew up. I don't get it."

"Sounds natural to me. Isn't that the way kids are. Don't want to break the umbilical cord?"

"Yeah, but they never come see us. Once or twice a year, maybe. So, what's the big deal about selling the house?"

The bitterness in Susan's voice surprised Rachel. She was usually very protective of her two children and never revealed any resentment about behavior Rachel clearly recognized as neglect.

"Well, I'm sure they'll get over it, Susan. By the time the house is sold, probably."

"I don't know. Amy says it should sell quickly." She looked at Rachel with eyes that seemed to have glazed over something dark and murky. "I've asked her not to put the 'For Sale' sign up until after the wedding."

Rachel nodded.

"Kind of felt like it might put a pall over your wedding day. Like a funeral was going on or something like that. You know, right across the street, right in the middle of your happy day, this sign announcing to the whole world the end of something, the end of everything that . . ."

"Now, wait a minute, Susan. Get hold of yourself," Rachel said as she lay an ear of corn down and wiped her hands on a towel. She walked over to where Susan sat and laid a hand on her shoulder.

When George walked through the door, the scene stopped him in his tracks. Ralph sniffed briefly at Susan and then pulled George out to the courtyard with him. Rachel watched as the two found seats in the sun.

Susan didn't seem to notice them pass through the room. Rachel poured her a glass of water and sat in silence while she drank it.

"You know you don't have to go through with the sale if you don't want to," she said.

Susan frowned, as if Rachel had told her she could step out the back door and take off for the moon. Rachel knew her friend well enough not to press the issue.

Suddenly, high-pitched shrieks pierced the air, the front door banged open and little feet clattered down the front hall. "George is here, Mommy. George! George!" Mary called and then skidded to a halt in the kitchen, her face falling in disappointment when she discovered he wasn't in the room.

"Why don't you go out back and see who's out there," Rachel said as she opened the door for the child. Belle wasn't far behind her daughter, her face radiant with a joy that washed over the gloom that minutes ago had hung so heavily in the kitchen.

Rachel and Susan watched as the three fell into each other's arms. Ralph ran circles around them and yelped in excitement. Rachel and Susan stood, arms around each other, and drank in the scene like a tonic.

* * *

Rachel struggled with the decision of whether to eat in the kitchen or outside when John walked in the door. Sometimes, it was too much trouble to carry everything out to the deck, she thought, but this was, after all, a special occasion. George would enjoy the fresh air – or at least the city version of it.

"How's Ben doing?" she asked as John walked into the kitchen and scooped her up in a big hug.

"He's driving them nuts, he's feeling so good. What's going on here? Looks like you're getting ready for a picnic."

"Thought it would be fun to eat outside on the deck for a change."

"What can I do to help?"

Rachel handed John a damp cloth and asked him to wipe off the table and chairs. While she gathered the feast she'd bought at the deli onto a tray to be carted outside, Belle filled glasses with water.

"Where's Mary," she asked.

"She and George are upstairs in Ben's room. She's showing him all the toys and books."

Belle smiled with a look Rachel recognized as storybook

romance. What better way to a mother's heart than through her child, she thought.

John walked back into the kitchen and tossed the dirty cloth on the counter. "Everything's ready. Let's eat."

"Did I hear the magic words?" George asked, clomping into the kitchen with Mary riding on his shoulders. When he saw John, he scooped the little girl off and sat her down in one of the kitchen chairs so he could shake hands with John. "Sorry to hear about your grandson," he said. "What's the latest report?"

John gave him the same good news he'd shared with Rachel just a few minutes before. "I'm sure he'd love to see you while you're in town if you have time to stop by the hospital. He loves having visitors."

George promised he'd make time. Crowded around the round glass table, the group held hands and bowed their heads.

"Who wants to say grace?" Rachel asked.

"I do," John said, surprising Rachel with his eagerness.

She looked over at Belle and saw her raised eyebrows. What's this all about, she wondered. She and John had never talked about their religious beliefs. She knew he was a godly man in the way he lived his life, always full of love and compassion, but whether he believed in some divine spirit to which he might pray was another matter. Within a few words, she had the answer to her question.

"Father in heaven," John began, "we thank You for each person gathered around this table and the blessings You have given each one of us. Especially thanks for Rachel and the way she has shared her home with each of us. Bless her as she has blessed us. And continue to be with Ben so that he can be with us again soon. Amen."

Ralph barked from under the table. Everybody laughed at what they all assumed was a doggie "amen" until he came charging out from under the table and ran to the wall that separated the courtyard from the street. There he leaped and barked so loudly that it was almost impossible to hear the banging on the front door.

Finally, Ricky's voice yelled above the knocking. "Belle, I know you're in there. Open up the door. Open up, or I'm going to raise some hell out here. I know he's in there. I know what you're up to."

Belle's face turned white, and she grabbed Mary out of her booster seat and into her arms. Tears formed in her eyes as she looked from Rachel to John, avoiding eye contact with George.

"Should I call the police?" Rachel asked as she bolted from her chair.

"No, let me go out there and see what he wants," John said.

"Want me to go with you?" George asked.

"No, I think you may be the problem, but thanks. In fact, why don't you all go on over next door until all this is over. I'll call when it's safe to come home."

"John's right," Rachel said. "Just leave everything right where it is and follow me."

She led the little group through the door in the brick wall that surrounded the courtyard and was relieved to see Mr. and Mrs. Moser peering out their dining room window. While Rachel was unable to see what was going on out front, she heard her front door open and was tempted to stay outside and listen to the drama. She knew that if she did, Belle would have the same idea, so she made herself mount the steps with the others. The back door was unlocked.

"What in the world is going on out there?" Mr. Moser asked, rushing into the kitchen as they entered. "Should we call the police? It's that fool, Ricky, again, isn't it?"

"Now, hush, honey," Mrs. Moser whispered, nodding toward Belle, who still held Mary in her arms as she tried to comfort the child.

Mary may not have remembered the night when Ricky showed up drunk, yelling for Belle as he stood out on the street in front of Rachel's house, but she knew something was wrong, and she clung to her mother's hair, twisting it in her little hands like a lifeline.

"Mommy?" she whimpered. "Why is Daddy yelling? Why is he mad? Maybe he needs me? Maybe . . ."

"No, baby. He doesn't need you. This has nothing to do with you. John is out there talking to him now. Everything's going to be all right. Remember when Ralph was lost, and we all worried so much, and then he came home?"

"Yes, I 'member."

"Well, this is going to be all right, too. Come on, let's go down to the basement and find the toys Mrs. Moser has for you."

As soon as the two disappeared down the steps, Mr. Moser picked up the phone and dialed 911. "Better to be safe than sorry," he told the others.

Ricky still ranted, although the words were so slurred nobody could understand what he yelled. Then banging metal echoed down the street.

"Oh, God, your truck," Rachel said, looking at George.

He headed toward the front door, but Belle held him back. "Please don't go out there, George. Please. Let the police handle this."

Rachel looked out the window and felt relieved to see that John had retreated inside her house. Probably to call the police, too. She cringed as Ricky raised a bent golf club over his head and crashed it down again onto the red truck. The windshield and both side mirrors were already either cracked or broken. Glass splinters covered the sidewalk. The sound of approaching sirens stopped Ricky in mid-swing. He seemed to hesitate for half a second, then dropped the club and disappeared down the street toward the Circle before the first police car pulled up in front of Rachel's house.

Rachel saw John step out onto the front porch to greet the officers. George turned to her.

"You stay here with Belle and Mary," he said. "They'll need you."

191

Rachel nodded. "Sorry about this, George. City life isn't always this violent."

George smiled but didn't look convinced.

Chapter Twenty-Three

hen Rachel realized that John and George had followed
the police to the station to file a complaint, she left
immediately for the hospital to check on Ben. John had
not exaggerated when he said the child had driven the nurses crazy.
When she arrived, she saw that he had created a teepee with books
piled up under the sheets. He sat under them, legs crossed Indian-
style.

When he saw Rachel, he yelled out, "Who goes there?"

"It's me. Rachel. What are you doing under there, Ben?"

"Do you have clearance to enter the reservation? Say the magic
word."

"I most certainly do have clearance, and I don't have to say the
magic word. Do you have clearance to be hiding under there? What
in the world are we going to do with you? I think it's definitely time
for you to come home."

At those words, Ben sprang out from under the tent of sheets and
leaped off the bed. Fortunately, Rachel caught him before he hit the
floor. "Careful there, big boy. This is a hospital, remember."

"When? When can I go home? I want to see George."

"George will be by to see you first thing tomorrow. And I'll talk
to the doctor as soon as I can and ask when she's going to release
you. We don't want to jump the gun and make you worse, do we?"

"Mary wasn't in the hospital this long," Ben pouted, hitting the
bed with his fist. "I want to go home now."

"I know you do, Ben, but we have to do what the doctor tells us."

"If my Mommy was here, she'd take me home now. She would. You just don't want me there. You don't love me. You just want Granddaddy all to yourself." Ben burst into wailing and buried his head under the pillows.

"What's going on here?" the head nurse asked as she rushed over to the bed.

"Ben wants to go home," Rachel said. "Now. I explained we have to follow the doctor's orders, but I'm afraid . . ."

"Ben, please take your head out from under the pillow so I can check your temperature," the nurse ordered. She looked at Rachel sympathetically as Ben began to beat his feet against the bed rails.

"Ben, please," Rachel said. "The nurse is trying to help you get better so you can go home. We all want you there. Ralph misses you."

At the sound of the dog's name, the kicking and crying stopped, and Ben reappeared from under the pillow.

"I'll try to get Dr. Cox to stop by as soon as possible," the nurse said. "How long will you be here?"

"As long as it takes to get to see her."

"I'll see what I can do." The nurse left the room, and Ben stopped crying but looked like he might start again at any moment.

"Ben, I know this is very, very hard for you, being here like this, away from your grandfather and . . ."

"And Ralph."

"And Ralph. You've been such a big boy through it all, and everybody's so proud of you. It's almost over now. You'll be going home soon, I promise, so hang on just a little longer, okay?"

Ben stuck his lower lip out but nodded his head. Rachel patted his knee. "Want to meditate a little with me? We can prop the pillows up, and you can sit on one just like a zafu. Want to try?"

Ben's face broke into a bright smile. "Yeah. I bet nobody, NOBODY, has ever done that before, don't you bet?"

194

"I bet you're right, Ben. And I bet if we meditate together, it will help you get better even faster."

Ben's eyes shut tight as he perched up on the pillows. Rachel sat on the bed beside him, which was where they were when Dr. Cox walked in.

"Sorry to interrupt," she said after standing for several minutes to survey the unusual scene in front of her.

"Look who it is, Ben. Dr. Cox. Can you say, hi, and tell her how you're feeling?"

"I'm feeling GREAT, and I want to go home NOW."

Dr. Cox consulted Ben's chart, walked around to the side of the bed to take a closer look at her patient and patted him on the head. "Well, you look great, and your tests all look great. The nurses say you've been pretty rambunctious, so I think maybe you're right. Think you can wait until tomorrow so we can get all the paperwork in order?"

Ben started to complain, but Rachel stopped him. "George is sleeping in your bed tonight, remember. I'll get him moved to the other bed tomorrow, but you wouldn't want him to feel confused by having to switch beds on the very first night he arrives, would you? That wouldn't be very nice."

Ben didn't look like he completely bought into that reasoning, but he didn't argue.

"And we need time to pack up all your stuff here. Look at all these toys and flowers. I'll tell you what. I'll take some home now, and we'll get the rest tomorrow."

"Early tomorrow?"

"Very early tomorrow," Rachel said as she leaned over to hug the boy.

He pressed his little mouth close to her ear and whispered, "I'm sorry I yelled at you, Rachel. I'm sorry I said what I did about you and Granddad. I didn't really mean it, you know."

"I know you didn't, Ben. Sometimes people say all kinds of

195

things they don't mean when they're unhappy. It's okay. When that happens, and we say we're sorry, the other person – the person who loves us – just has to let it go."

"Did you let it go?"

"I let it go, Ben."

"Guess that means you love me, right?"

Rachel smiled and tousled his hair. "That's what it means."

* * *

When John knocked on her bedroom door, Rachel dropped her book and called to him to come in. As he propped himself up on the pillows beside her, he sighed deeply. The two sat in silence for several minutes before he spoke.

"What's the book?"

"*The Forbidden Garden.*"

"Thought you'd already read it."

"I had read it and loved it, which is why I'm reading it again."

John leaned over and kissed her nose. "Thanks for stopping by to stay with Ben while I was at the police station. Sounds like things got a little hairy. You ready for his homecoming tomorrow?"

"You know I am. I've missed him. But, tell me what happened to Ricky. And where's George?"

John launched into the story of Ricky's arrest for property damage, resisting arrest, public drunkenness and assault with a deadly weapon.

"Assault with a deadly weapon? What in the world do you mean?"

"The golf club. He took a swing at the police officer with it."

"Oh, dear. That poor man."

"These things happen when you're falling down drunk. They practically poured him into the cruiser."

Rachel had walked out to look at George's truck before the tow truck had dragged it away and knew that the insurance company would deem it a total loss. "What's George going to do now?"

"Rent a car, I guess. Right now he and Belle have things other than transportation on their minds. She's pretty upset about Ricky, and he's downstairs trying to comfort her."

"I spent a few minutes with her earlier. She did a good job of holding herself together for Mary's sake, but I could tell she was having a hard time. She cares about Ricky, and I think she had high hopes he was getting his life on the right track."

"I imagine she's embarrassed that George saw this, not to mention that we all had to go through it a second time. What do you think will happen now to Ricky?"

"Did he call a lawyer?"

"He was passed out when I left. Doesn't he work in a law firm?"

"That's right. I suspect one of them may step up to the bat and spring him."

"Maybe. But right now, let's stop talking about Ricky and Belle and George and focus on you and me a little."

"Do you need to be focused on?"

"I need to be focused on. A lot."

* * *

Rachel stopped by her office early the next morning to check with Georgia before she went to the hospital with John. Georgia looked up from her computer when her boss walked in.

"Well, hello, stranger. I was worried you might have forgotten where you worked."

"I knew you could handle things here. In fact, you handle things here so well, I'm really thinking more and more about retiring and leaving the firm to you."

"Right. Now that you've got a man to support you, you're just going to jump ship. Happens all the time."

"On second thought, what would I do without your chocolate chip cookies?" Rachel picked up a pile of pink message slips and leafed through them. One from Carrie had "URGENT" written on it in big, capital letters at the top.

"Do you know what this is about?"

"No. She called from her cellphone, and I had a lot of trouble hearing her. About all I got for sure was the "urgent" part."

Rachel leafed through the rest of the stack Georgia had numbered in order of importance and dialed Carrie's cellphone. Carrie answered on the first ring.

"Rachel, thanks for calling back so quickly. How's Ben?"

"We're bringing him home today. I just stopped by the office for a few minutes before heading to the hospital. Georgia said you needed to talk to me. What's going on?"

"Let me close the door. Hang on." Rachel heard a click as the door closed and waited for Carrie to speak. "Rachel, I've got a real problem. Horace Junior has a huge fan club here. I've had a revolving door ever since the announcement was made that I'm taking over and he's leaving. Half the staff is threatening to quit. Honestly, I don't know what to do."

"Have you spoken to Horace?"

"We're not talking. I can't believe he's acting like this. Like a spoiled child who's had his favorite toy taken away."

"What I can't believe is that he would let his father's dream go under because he's gotten his feelings hurt. Horace worked so hard to build his business, and his son watched him do it. Unless maybe that's what's going on. Maybe he resented all the time Horace spent at work, and this is his way of getting revenge."

"Surely not."

"I've seen stranger things happen in the world of business, believe me."

"But he's hurting himself if the business goes under. He's a stockholder. He'll lose money."

"Sometimes the hurt little boy emotions are stronger than the adult's rational needs."

Carrie didn't respond for nearly a minute and then spoke in her own childish voice. "So, what am I supposed to do? Just sit back and watch the hurt little boy trash the company?"

"Give him some time. I think the less you do in reaction the better. I'll draft a company memo from you that you can send to all your employees. In fact, I'll work on it tonight so you can send it out tomorrow. I'd follow it up with a staff meeting. And, Carrie, are you willing to invest some money on this?"

"What exactly do you mean?"

"Incentives to stay. Bonuses."

"I don't know whether the company can afford to give enough to make it worth their staying."

"Then maybe it's time to clean house. There are lots of people out there looking for jobs. Maybe you should hold a job fair. Get some new blood."

"I don't know, Rachel. Sounds scary."

"Think about it overnight. I will, too. Why don't I meet you in your office tomorrow morning early. Before your employees arrive. We'll make a game plan and get it going right away. Don't worry in the meantime. I have a feeling everything's going to work out just fine."

When Rachel ended the call, Georgia walked in to let her know that John waited on the other line. "Are you ready for me to pick you up, madam?" he asked.

"Can you give me about fifteen more minutes? Georgia had a stack of phone messages waiting for me, and some of them really need my attention."

"You don't need to go with me, you know. I can pick up Ben by myself, and we'll be all settled in by the time you get home."

"I think you've forgotten how much stuff there is in his room to be brought home."

"Belle offered to go with me, and, actually, helping with Ben might take her mind off Ricky."

"What about Mary?"

"George said he'd take care of Mary. I think they're getting ready to take Ralph for a walk right now."

"Well, if you're sure. I don't want Ben to think anything is more important to me than his coming home."

"Don't worry, Rachel. Ben knows how much you love him. And seriously, I think going with me would help Belle let go of some of the guilt she feels about last night. When she walked upstairs a little while ago to see George, she didn't look like she'd slept much last night."

Rachel finally agreed with the plan for Belle to go with John and said she'd see them around lunchtime. That would give her time to return the phone calls and get started on a rough draft of the memo for Carrie. When she walked out to the lobby to tell Georgia of her change of plans, she saw her secretary staring at her computer screen with a scowl on her face.

"What is it?" Rachel asked as she walked around the corner of the desk to see what had disturbed Georgia.

"Isn't that Chelsea?" Georgia asked, pointing to a picture of a girl who had been found dead. The headline read "Metro suicide." Rachel nodded her head and read the news report. The young woman had thrown herself in front of a metro train at the Dupont Circle stop. Georgia stroked her hand. "You can't save them all, Rachel."

Chapter Twenty-Four

D on't be too hard on yourself," Georgia said, trying to comfort her boss. "I can see what's going through your head right now."

Rachel told Georgia about her conversation with Ricky just the week before. "He said he'd try to get her to an NA meeting."

"Yes, but Ricky isn't doing too well himself. That was sort of like the blind leading the blind."

"Maybe I should have had her involuntarily committed. Maybe — "

"Rachel, stop."

Rachel handed her the stack of pink message slips. "Do me a favor. Call these people and tell them there's been a death in the family and that I'm taking a few days off. I've got to get down to the Circle and find Deejee. This must be horrible for her. First Ricky gets locked up and now this."

Georgia nodded and stuffed some chocolate chip cookies in a plastic bag. "Take these home to Ben and tell him I'll stop by this weekend to check on him. And, Rachel, take care of yourself. You worry me."

"Don't worry. Call."

Rachel picked up her briefcase and left before Georgia could protest any more. As she walked toward Dupont Circle and the hotdog stand where she was sure she'd find her friend, Deejee, she thought about the day she had met Chelsea.

Ralph, as in so many cases, had brought together the 62-year-old lawyer and the teen living on the street. It was Ralph who had gotten through Chelsea's hard shell. Over time, Rachel had looked forward to their visits at the Circle. When Ralph disappeared, Chelsea had led the search. The experience had forged a special bond between Rachel and the girl.

When Rachel found her hunkered down in a heap in a corner of the metro station, stoned out of her mind and doing nothing to hide the needle marks on her arms, she felt like someone had hit her in the stomach. Chelsea refused to admit she was using again. Rachel's only hope had been Ricky's willingness, as a fellow addict, to do what he could to help the girl. Now she was dead.

Rachel turned the corner and was relieved to see Deejee at her regular spot. As she drew closer, Rachel knew she had heard the news. Instead of standing in her "let me serve you a hotdog" stance, she sat slumped in a lawn chair.

"Guess you heard?"

"Just now."

Deejee shook her head. "Ain't no hope sometimes, Rachel. No hope."

"Were you here when it happened?"

"Got here just as they were bringing her body up. What was left of it."

Rachel gasped. "You saw her?"

Deejee nodded. "I identified the body. One of the cops knew we were friends."

"Where is she now?"

"Took her down to the city morgue. No family. Nothing to claim anyway. She was living on the streets."

"I'd like to see that the body is taken care of."

Deejee nodded.

"What's the word on Ricky? I've been so focused on getting Ben home and keeping tabs on the office, I haven't checked at the station."

"One of the lawyers at the firm where he's at bailed him out and got him to agree to go to rehab. I think the firm's paying for it. Twenty-eight-day program. Don't guess we'll have to worry about ole Ricky for a while. Guess he just couldn't handle the thought of Belle and Mary with another man."

"I'm sorry. He seemed to be doing so well."

"A little early in his recovery for such a change in his life. Losing the only family he had."

"Well, it's not like he'd lost them, Deejee. Belle and George just met."

Deejee shook her head and sighed but didn't say a word. She sat in silence. Finally, she looked up at Rachel and smiled sadly. "He knew, Rachel. He knew."

* * *

When Rachel opened the door, Ralph rushed out and barked as if he sensed something. Sensed that Ben was coming home. Sensed that Chelsea was dead. Sensed all kinds of other things that Rachel didn't even know. Yet.

"Calm down, boy. We need to get a few things settled here before everybody gets back." Rachel waited outside with Ralph while he made his rounds and then realized something was wrong. "I thought George and Mary were going to take you for a walk. What happened?"

Ralph gave one more bark and then dashed to the side of the house and down the steps toward the basement apartment. Rachel followed him and had just reached the bottom step when George opened the door.

"Well, hello," he said. "We were on our way up. Mary had a nosebleed, and our plan to walk Ralph got a little delayed." Mary sat on the sofa with her head tilted back. "You about ready to try it again, Missy?"

Mary nodded and very gingerly eased off the sofa and walked

toward the door. "George fixed me," she said, smiling at Rachel as though she'd just witnessed a miracle. Brain surgery, maybe.

"Yes, it sure looks like he did. Why don't you run on up there with Ralph while I talk to George a minute." At the mention of the dog's name, Mary flew out the door and bounded up the stairs. Rachel shared the news about Chelsea's death and Ricky's trip to rehab.

"As soon as John gets back with Ben and we get him settled in, I'm going to go down to make arrangements for the body. She didn't have any family. Will you tell Belle about Ricky? She needs to know he's out of jail."

"Sure, I can do that. But right now, I'm going to do what I promised Mary we'd do. Take Ralph for a walk. Sure you don't want to join us?"

"No. I'll wait here for the boys. They should be home soon. You all have fun. And, George . . ."

George turned around. "Yes?"

"Thanks."

"For what?"

"Everything."

* * *

Rachel had barely hung the "Welcome home, Ben" banner Susan made when John drove up. She hammered the final tack in the bed sheet sprayed with bright glittery letters and turned as a car door slammed. And then another, followed by the pattering of feet running up the walk.

"Hey, slow down there, buddy. You just got out of the hospital, remember. If you don't want to go back, you need to take it easy, like Dr. Cox told you."

"Where's Ralph?" Ben asked in a forced subdued voice.

"Where's Mary?"

Rachel laughed and wrapped her arms around him in a big hug, just as he caught sight of the sign.

"Wow! Cool," he squealed, breaking into a huge grin.

Susan dashed across the street to join in the welcome home festivities.

"Susan made the sign for you," John said. "Didn't she do a nice job?"

"Yeah, I knowed it was Susan. You and Rachel don't color too good."

Rachel and John laughed. "Well, maybe not, but Rachel's got your room all ready for you, so let's go upstairs, and you can lie down and wait for Ralph to come back from his walk. I'll come up with you."

"I'm going over and take care of the business with Chelsea," Rachel said. "I'll be back for supper."

"I've got that all taken care of," Susan said. "Baked lasagna and a blueberry pie. Enough for an army. I'll bring it over at five."

Rachel hugged her friend. "What will I do when you're gone?"

"Maybe you all should come with us. The beach can always use another lawyer."

"What about me?" John asked.

"You, sir, can just relax. Retire with us, and let Rachel support you. That woman loves to work. Enough for all of us, in fact. I keep telling her 'Slow down, you're going to have a heart attack,' but does she slow down? Not on your life. Just the other day . . ."

"Okay, okay, we get your point," Rachel interrupted. "Thanks for supper. See you at five." She kissed everybody and stepped out on the curb to hail a cab.

"Do you want me to go with you?" Susan asked. "Could be grim. Nobody should have to do 'grim' by themselves."

"You may be right. Come on."

The two hopped in the back seat of a Yellow Cab that roared off almost before they closed their doors.

"Where to, lady?"

"The city morgue."

The cab driver sank into appropriate silence when he heard the destination, and they rode in quiet for several blocks, until Susan couldn't stand it any longer.

"I know this probably isn't a good time to bring this up, Rachel, but you've been so hard to catch lately. And now that I have you here —"

"A captive audience."

"Yes, a captive audience," Susan giggled. "Let's talk about the wedding."

"My god, Susan, here we are on our way to the city morgue to make arrangements for a poor girl who probably killed herself, and you want to make wedding plans."

"It'll cheer us up. Going on with life. Ben's home and feeling good. I say we do it in two weeks. I won't have moved yet and can take care of Ben while you go on your honeymoon. Give me one good reason why you can't get married in two weeks?"

"Well, it's just so sudden."

"Rachel Springer, you had it all finalized and then canceled, remember? This is not the first go-around. Maybe we can even talk George into staying and helping us get things ready."

"I'm sure Belle would love that."

"And we need to go shopping for a dress for Belle. Has John got a tux?"

"I think so. Hold on. We're here. Let's table this until after we've taken care of Chelsea, okay?"

"But we've decided on the date, right? I can call the florist and the photographer and get the caterer back on track?"

"I guess."

"You guess?"

"Yes, Susan. Two weeks. But one thing."

"What?"

"I want George to take the pictures."

"Sure," Susan said and smiled as she leaped out of the car like she was going anywhere but to the city morgue.

As Rachel looked at her friend, dressed in a hot pink jogging suit, her heart skipped a few beats at the thought of her move.

Chapter Twenty-Five

O n her way home, Rachel fingered a piece of paper. The Narcotics Anonymous schedule had grown dirty, coffee-stained and torn in several places. Names – first names only – and phone numbers covered every available empty space.

"She really tried," Susan said. "You've got to give her that much. Nobody tried any harder."

Rachel nodded and tucked the schedule in her purse. When the body had been recovered from the metro tracks, the schedule had fallen out of a jacket pocket. There had been no money. An expired Florida driver's license had provided the only identification. Rachel called Stan and asked him to try to find Chelsea's family. Within several hours, he called back and said he'd located the girl's parents.

"They said do whatever you want with her stuff," he said. "She was dead to them a long time ago."

After some thought, Rachel instructed the morgue to donate the body to science. She felt her friend would have wanted that, especially if addiction studies would benefit. Maybe some good would come from such a tragic end.

She wondered whether she should call Ricky. She knew he had tried to help Chelsea, and, from the looks of the schedule, he'd gotten her to at least one NA meeting.

But getting in touch with Ricky presented another set of problems. Stan had told her that someone from the law firm where he worked had bailed him out and gotten him into rehab. For 28 days at least, they'd be free of Ricky.

"What are you thinking about?" Susan interrupted her. "Your face looks like a thundercloud."

"Ricky. What to do about Ricky."

"My goodness, girl, you barely get one problem taken care of, and you're on to the next. Can't you let Ricky alone for the next few weeks. He's being handled where he is. We've got other things better to —"

"I know, but I'm worried about Belle and how she might react to this whole turn of events. She took the news of Chelsea's death pretty hard, and I'm afraid she'll take Ricky back out of fear. Fear of what he'll do to himself. Think she can protect him."

"Just like you think you can protect Belle, you mean."

Rachel looked at her friend and felt like she'd been hit between the eyes with a slingshot. "This is definitely a case of a pot calling the kettle black," she laughed.

"But you know I'm right, don't you?"

"Ladies, I believe you live here, right?" the cabbie snapped.

Rachel realized they'd been sitting in front of her house with the meter running. "Sorry," she said as she handed the man a twenty dollar bill. "Thanks. Keep the change."

Ralph ran to the curb to welcome them, Ben and Mary right behind him.

"Hey, guys," Susan said. "Ben, I hope you're taking it easy. You don't want to end up back in the hospital."

Ben looked very serious and assured the adults that he'd been resting ever since they had left. "Granddad said we could take Ralph out for a short walk to the end of the sidewalk. He needed fresh air."

"George," Mary squealed and dashed off down the street to meet her mother and George, laden down with shopping bags.

As the two got closer, Rachel saw the smiles. They looked like children coming home from a trip to the candy store.

"What in the world? You look like you've robbed the mall.

What's all this?" Rachel asked.

George smiled. "This little lady sure likes to shop."

"Bargains. I like to find bargains. Susan, the sales today were unreal. And George is spoiling me rotten."

Susan looked at Rachel. "I don't think you've got a thing to worry about," she said.

* * *

Rachel sat on the sofa in the den, working on Carrie's employee plan when John walked in the room later that evening. He kissed her on the back of her neck, on the sweet spot under her braid.

"You look mighty serious. Like you're planning World War III."

"Actually, you're not far off. Carrie is having trouble at work, and I'm trying to come up with a damage control plan to save the company from the effects of Horace Junior. I'm supposed to meet her at her office early tomorrow morning."

"You look gorgeous when you're working. I love a smart woman."

"You're nuts," Rachel laughed. "How's Ben?"

"Sleeping like only the innocent can. So glad to be home. Ralph's at the foot of his bed, looking like he's in heaven."

John sat down on the sofa beside her, moving a pile of papers to the floor. "So, tell me, madam attorney, what can I do for you? I think it's time for us now. Work time, bedtime for little boys. All that's over, and now it's time for you and me. Don't you think? Rachel, I'm so glad things are back on track. What a rough few weeks we've had."

Laughter bubbled up through the floor from the basement apartment.

"Wow, I didn't realize you could hear so well what goes on down there," John said.

Rachel remembered her concern about sharing the house with him. When she told him about her fear that he might play a trumpet and keep her awake, he laughed.

"What about wild parties?"

"And wild women."

"You're the only wild woman I need. Soon as I met you —"

"And saw my impatiens plants . . ."

"And your impatiens plants. As soon as I saw them, I knew you were the one."

Rachel snuggled closer. "Susan wants to do the wedding in a couple of weeks. What do you think? If you think it's too early, I agree. We can put it off until Ben's really out of the woods more. Or maybe . . ."

"I think two weeks is perfect."

"Really?"

"Really. I can't wait to call you my wife. Mrs. Turner. Sounds so good to me."

"What about Springer & Associates?"

"What about it?"

"Do I need to change the name of the firm?"

"How about this," John chuckled. "Now you've finally got an associate."

* * *

Carrie paced the floor of her office the next morning. The woman had aged in the short time since Horace's death and the reading of the will. She had changed from a young woman in love and involved in a satisfying career to a woman who looked like she carried the weight of the world on her shoulders. Her eyes were ringed in dark shadows of loneliness.

As Rachel opened the office door, Carrie stood still and straight.

She didn't speak. She looked like she hadn't slept the night before. Rachel walked toward her and laid her briefcase on the table next to a chair. She clicked open the latches. "Shall we get down to work?" she asked, all business.

Carrie sat in the chair next to hers without a word. She folded her hands in her lap, her back ramrod straight.

"Horace left his company to you, Carrie, because he knew you were smart and he knew you were strong. He knew you were like him."

"But he didn't know the employees would react the way they have."

"Yes, I think he probably knew that Horace Junior would do exactly what he did and that he would have followers."

"Then, why would he jeopardize the company by leaving me in charge?"

"I think he did it because he knew you could handle it." Rachel pulled out a document she had drafted the night before and handed it to Carrie. The speech to be read to the employees in a company meeting that morning was short and to the point. It outlined a plan that included incentives for employees who committed to stay with the company under Carrie's leadership. Those who aligned themselves with Horace Junior were offered a severance package that was generous but nowhere near the bonuses for those who stayed.

"Do you think this will work?"

"I think it will weed out some employees who probably needed to leave anyway. I think Horace would approve."

Carrie took a few minutes to read through the pages and straightened her shoulders. "What about Horace Junior?"

"Sorry, dear, but that's something you'll have to handle on your own. Affairs of the heart aren't so easily managed."

Carrie tapped her pen on the desk and looked out the window at the parking lot which had begun to fill with cars as employees arrived for work.

"Want me to stay and attend the meeting with you? There may be questions."

"Will you?"

"Sure. Just let me call Georgia and tell her I'll be a little late. And while I'm doing that, you need to make enough copies of this agreement for all your employees."

Carrie left the room with the form, and Rachel sat down at the desk to call her office. She was surprised when Georgia answered. "What are you doing there?"

"I work here, remember?"

"Yes, but it's early." Rachel looked at her watch. "Georgia, it's not even eight o'clock yet. What are you doing at work before eight o'clock?"

"I woke up early and decided I might as well come on in and get some stuff done before the phone starts ringing. And if what Susan tells me is true, we've got a lot to get done in the next couple of weeks."

"I can't believe this. Do you mean to tell me that Susan has called you and told you already?"

"I'm in charge of getting the caterer back on track."

"That Susan is too much."

"Is that why you called, cause if not, get to the point. I've got things to do here."

"I called to tell you I'm going to be late. Carrie wants me at the meeting with her this morning. It could be ten o'clock or later by the time I get in."

"No problem. Your first appointment is at eleven. Take your time. I'll be here. Now let me off the phone so I can call the caterer."

* * *

The meeting was short. A handful of employees chose to leave with Horace Junior to start a new venture. Those who decided to stay were grateful for the incentive bonus. When Rachel left to return to her office, the mood in the conference room felt like a revival meeting. In a way, it is a revival, she thought. Horace would be proud of the way Carrie handled herself. And probably not surprised in the least by his son's immature behavior.

Rachel still chuckled to herself when she walked into her office.

"What's got you so tickled?" Georgia asked. "I thought you'd been through World War III."

"Nothing's ever as bad as you think it's going to be."

Georgia handed her the dreaded pile of telephone messages. "Anything urgent here? I thought I'd lie down and take a quick power nap before my first appointment."

"A call from Susan."

"Of course, she thinks it's urgent, right?" Georgia nodded. "Okay, I'll call her back, but after that, please hold all my calls so I can clear my head for a bit."

"Good luck," Georgia said with a sly grin.

"What is it? You know why she's calling, don't you."

"Maybe."

"Tell me. Don't make me face her unprepared."

"Go ahead. You'll be fine. And I'll be right out here at my desk if you need me."

Susan answered on the first ring. "Rachel?"

"Yes, it's me. What is it?"

"The most horrible thing has happened. Are you sitting down?"

Rachel sat down. "Yes."

"Somebody's made an offer on our house." Rachel sucked in her breath. "Did you hear me?"

"Yes, but I just can't believe it. It's so fast. The market's down.

Nobody's buying houses these days."

"Well, there's one person who is, and he's buying mine and offered full price, and he wants to move in here in thirty days."

"So soon?"

"Two weeks after the wedding."

"Who is it?"

"A young couple with children. They saw the swing set Jim made for the grandchildren and fell in love even before they came inside. And Ben was outside with Ralph. I think Ralph was the deal-maker."

"He always is."

"Well, I wanted you to be the first to know."

"So, you've already signed the purchase offer?"

"They're paying cash. Jim says we need to accept before they have second thoughts."

"Yeah. I guess there's no reason to prolong the matter. You decided to sell. Now, you've got a buyer."

"Right. No reason to think any more about it. But, Rachel ..."

"Yes?"

"Oh, nothing. See you later."

"See you later, Susan." Rachel hung up the phone and thought about how she wouldn't be saying those words much longer. "See you later." It had such a nice ring. "See you later" might mean in a few minutes or in a few days, but it had such hope. After Susan moved to the beach "later" could mean months. Now the "see you" part might mean catching a glimpse of Susan outside in the early morning hours in her ratty blue bathrobe to get the paper. Soon, some stranger would live across the street and maybe not even get the paper. Rachel felt tears well up and walked over to shut her door. She lay down on the sofa and closed her eyes.

What will this do to Ben, she wondered. Susan had become like a second mother to him. She didn't have an answer. So many dilemmas didn't have answers. Years later, looking back, sometimes things made sense. She wondered if this would.

Chapter Twenty-Six

A fter Rachel finished stacking the supper dishes in the dishwasher and wiped off the countertops, she turned to John and Ben sitting at the table working on a jigsaw puzzle together. The sight of their two heads bent over the project – one a grayer version of the other. A warmth spread inside her. She smiled and walked over to stand closer to the two people who had become so important in her life. A year ago, she hadn't even known them, she realized. Life's gifts come when and how we least expect them, she thought. She picked up a puzzle piece and fit it in the middle of the lighthouse.

Ben looked up at her, his eyes huge. "How did you do that?" he shouted. "I've been looking for that piece for hours."

"I told you she's smart," John said. "That's why I'm marrying her. She's a smart lady."

"And she's nice, too."

"Yes, very nice."

"You guys look like you're doing pretty well without me. I'm going downstairs to talk to Belle for a few minutes. I'll be back before your bedtime, Ben. Don't forget to brush your teeth."

"Ricky?" John asked.

Rachel nodded. "She needs to know. To be prepared."

"Don't be long. I've got a surprise for you when you get back."

"A surprise!" Ben squealed. "Let's give it to her now. Is there one for me, too?"

"No, Ben. This is a woman kind of surprise you wouldn't have any interest in at all." Ben's mouth pursed in a pout. "Okay, come here, and I'll whisper in your ear what it is."

Ben jumped off the chair and rushed around to John's side of the table where John cupped his hands around his ear and whispered. Ben nodded his head. "He's right," he said to Rachel. "It's a woman thing," and went back to the puzzle.

Rachel laughed and kissed John. "I won't be long. I like woman things." She let herself out the back door. The motion sensor came on, lighting her way around the side of the house to the steps leading down to the basement apartment.

She knocked and heard little feet run toward her. Mary threw open the door and launched herself into Rachel's arms, almost knocking her off balance.

"Careful there, little missy. You don't want to land Rachel in the hospital right here so soon before her big day," George said.

Rachel stepped inside the little living room still filled with the smell of the fried chicken Belle had served for supper. A few crumbs stuck to Mary's upper lip, and Rachel laughed at the sheer joy of the scene before her. She hated to say anything that might introduce a black cloud of worry into Belle's life. She hesitated only a minute and then did what she had come to do.

"Mary, would you like to run upstairs and help John and Ben with their jigsaw puzzle? They need a girl's touch."

"Can George go, too?"

"Maybe he should walk up there with you, but then I need him back down here for a few minutes while I talk to your Mommy."

Relieved that she wouldn't have to walk through the dark alone, Mary grabbed George's hand. As they closed the door behind them, Belle turned a worried look toward her friend.

"It's Ricky, isn't it?"

Rachel nodded. "He's out of jail and in a rehab center. I called to leave a message about Chelsea, but he still can't take calls. He'll be there 28 days."

"If he stays."

George walked in, took one look at Belle's face and rushed over to take her in his arms. The three sat in silence, the tick of the clock echoing around them.

"Ricky's out of jail," Belle whispered.

"But he's in rehab, Belle, and we can hope that he's getting the help he needs this time."

"The news about Chelsea won't help."

Rachel's heart lurched. Had she done the wrong thing by calling to let him know? Maybe they wouldn't give him the message if they thought the news would be too disturbing. Maybe . . .

"They were so close. He'll feel responsible," Belle said.

"But the counselors there will know how to help him deal with his feelings," George said. "Rachel did the right thing. He needed to know, and it was better that he find out while he's got plenty of support to help him with his reactions." He hugged Belle closer to him, looking over her head at Rachel with a reassuring smile.

What a good, wise man Belle has found, she thought. What a gift they are to each other.

"How are you doing, honey?" George asked the woman leaning limply against his chest.

Belle sat silently for so long Rachel wondered if she would answer the question. Finally, the one word – "afraid" – came out in barely a whisper.

"Afraid of what?" George coaxed her.

"Afraid he won't stay. Afraid he'll do something and get kicked out. Afraid he'll stay but come out the same sick man he was when he went in. I'm afraid . . ."

"What, honey? Go ahead and get it all out."

Belle began to weep great heaving sobs that came from deep within her. Years of fear – and the burden of having to hide those fears from Mary – poured out onto George's broad chest. Rachel watched as he sat and held her, silently, strongly, supporting her body as it released so much pain. Rachel wondered if she should leave and made a move toward the door, but George shook his head.

"She needs us both. Stay," he said.

After what seemed like a very long time – but which, in fact, was only minutes – Belle's sobbing stopped abruptly. George handed her a red bandana, and she wiped her face with it. She laughed when she handed the soaked wad of material back to him.

"You may want to throw that away. It's probably toxic."

"Actually, I thought I might use it as a wall hanging so you can look at it and rejoice at what you've been able to let go. The past. Ricky can't hurt you anymore. You've just washed him all away. Doesn't matter whether he stays in rehab or not, or what he does when he gets out. He can't hurt you anymore because he's not part of you anymore. He's gone."

Rachel thought of the pictures of the Vietnamese children on the walls of George's house at the farm. She thought of the pain he had experienced and learned to let go. She remembered the magic tower of rocks in the river, and she prayed that Belle would find the same release.

She saw the way the two of them looked at each other and knew it was time for her to leave. She hoped she could do what George suggested. Her years as a lawyer made worrying as normal as breathing. In addition to all the fears Belle had listed, her own experience dealing with drunks had given her opportunities to add a few more of her own. As she looked over at the smile on Belle's face as she relaxed in George's arms, she decided she'd better head back upstairs before her own toxic thoughts poisoned the other two.

"I'll have Ben walk Mary back down in a few minutes. You two enjoy some alone time," she said.

Rachel heard the deadbolt lock as she got to the top of the stairs.

* * *

"I got a piece! I got a piece," Mary shouted as Rachel walked into the kitchen. Ben looked at the little girl proudly and nodded his head.

"Mary said she'd be my sister," he told Rachel. "She really needs a big brother, don't you think, Rachel?"

"I think that's a wonderful idea, Ben." Rachel tried not to think of the future. Of the possibility that Belle would someday move to the farm with George, and Ben would face another loss. She hadn't told him yet about Susan's move but hoped that the children who would soon live across the street would soften the blow.

"Everything okay downstairs?" John asked.

Rachel nodded and started to share her gratitude for George's support when the phone rang. On the other end of the line, her cousin Nancy wanted to know how she could help with the wedding. She grew quiet when Rachel told her all the food was being catered, and it took a lot of talking to convince her that all she had to do was find someone to milk the cows so she and Simon could join the wedding party.

"And don't forget you did the biggest part by helping me find my grandmother's dress."

Rachel knew she would get several more phone calls in the next two weeks to make sure there wasn't something from the farm she needed.

"How are you all getting along without George?" she asked. "He sure seems comfortable here for someone who says he hates the city."

"Simon is handling things fine, but we hope George will come back at least for a few days between now and the wedding. We've got someone coming to talk about buying some cattle from us, and we need his advice. Have him give us a call when he has a chance."

Rachel said she would and hung up the phone.

"Ready for your surprise now?" John asked.

"Can I go get it for her?" Ben asked.

"Me, too?" Mary whispered as she hopped up and down beside her new big brother.

"Think you two can manage it? It's pretty big and heavy."

Ben laughed and grabbed Mary's hand. In a stage whisper Rachel heard across the room, he said, "He's joking. He's just trying to fool her."

The two children ran up the stairs together, and Rachel sat down on John's lap. "What's this all about?"

"Just be patient, and you'll see." He nuzzled her ear with the stubble of his beard, tickling her so she squirmed.

"Hah! Caught you!" Ben shouted. "Caught you getting ready to smooch, didn't we!"

He thrust a small package at Rachel. The box had been wrapped in silver paper and tied with a lavender silk bow. It was almost too beautiful to open, she thought. Mary didn't feel the same hesitation and offered to help.

"No, this is a very special gift for Rachel. You let her do it," John said as he reached down to take Mary's chubby little hands off the bow.

Seeing the tears well up in the child's eyes, Rachel patted her tiny shoulder and told her she could have the bow when Rachel took it off. Mary smiled, and Rachel continued to open her gift slowly. A gold locket on a delicate chain lay inside on layers of white tissue paper.

"Oh, John, it's beautiful," Rachel said as she lifted the piece of jewelry out of the box to admire it. She started to open the clasp and put it around her neck, but John stopped her.

"No, this is for you to wear on our wedding day. It was my mother's – a gift from my father to her the day they got married." He turned over the locket to show Rachel two inscriptions. His parents' initials and wedding date and, beneath it, their own.

"I thought about waiting to give it to you on the day of the wedding, but I was afraid things would be so hectic that I'd forget. Do you mind?"

"That's not true," Ben shouted. "He just couldn't wait, could you, Granddad?"

Rachel laughed and looked at John. "No, Granddad doesn't like to wait." Rachel smiled. "But he does a pretty good job when he has to."

Chapter Twenty-Seven

The next few weeks flew by as Rachel knew they would. George returned to the farm, with the promise that he'd be back the day before the wedding. He and Belle planned to help Susan take care of Ben since she had her hands full with all the packing that had to be done. At times, Rachel felt she was in the middle of a whirlwind. Every time Susan saw Rachel at home, she ran across the street with some wedding detail that needed to be discussed.

"You'd think we were having a huge church wedding with hundreds of guests instead of a little living room affair with 25 people," Rachel said to Georgia as they sat in her office going over her calendar for the next couple of weeks. Georgia had managed to postpone court dates and put off scheduled appointments so Rachel and John could have a week's honeymoon and another week at home before she started back to work.

"Do you know where you're going on your honeymoon yet?"

"No, John won't tell me anything except that I should bring sunscreen."

"And you're okay with that? You, Miss Control Freak. I can't believe it."

"Well, believe it. Actually, I'm really enjoying letting him do all the planning and arranging and worrying."

"Not everybody worries the way you do, Rachel. Some people just schedule the flights, book the room and relax."

"Really?"

"Really. So you'll call me as soon as you have a number where I can reach you, right?"

Rachel laughed. "Now, who's worrying?"

Georgia smiled sheepishly. "Well, somebody's got to be responsible for the office, Boss Lady."

The two sat in comfortable silence. Georgia finally rose, disappeared into the lobby and returned with a plate of chocolate chip cookies.

"I don't know, Georgia. I'm trying not to gain any weight. My grandmother was a tiny woman, and her dress is already tight."

Georgia broke a cookie and handed Rachel her half. "Walk around the desk a couple of times while you're eating it, and the calories won't stick."

"That's why I hired you, Georgia Payne. You always have a solution."

Georgia chewed her cookie, looking wise. "I'll miss you, Rachel Springer. This will be our first long separation, you know. First time since I started working for you. You are coming back, aren't you?"

Rachel stopped in mid-bite. "Why, Georgia, did you really think you could get rid of me?"

"Stranger things have happened."

"This strange thing won't happen. We've got too much left to do together."

And, as if to accentuate her point, Rachel took another cookie off the plate and stuffed the whole thing in her mouth.

* * *

The day of the wedding dawned with clear skies, as wedding days should. A gentle breeze stirred the air. Birdsong woke Rachel, and she smiled. She lay in bed, luxuriating in the quiet of the morning. As usual, she woke before anyone else. She listened to the

225

house breathe, as old houses do. A creak here, a groan there, and she chuckled as she remembered how the noises frightened her when she first moved in. Now all the settling noises comforted her as if the old house were alive, telling her "good morning." Wishing her an especially good morning on her wedding day.

She sat up and glanced around the room she'd share with John when they returned from Taos. She had stumbled upon the airline tickets to Albuquerque and, beside them, the confirmation for their reservation at the Mabel Dodge Luhan House. While disappointed that she no longer had a surprise to look forward to, she was excited about sharing her favorite places in Taos with John. Doc Martin's, Café Tazzo, Ojo Caliente. The tarot reader who had told her years ago about the dog she would find and that many things would change as a result.

Many things had, she thought as she climbed the stairs to her third floor meditation room. As she sat down on the zafu and arranged a blanket around her shoulders, the deep breath she took felt deeper than usual. As if some place had been carved out inside her, waiting to be filled. Rachel smiled and let out her breath slowly. Ralph scratched on the door and interrupted her meditation. When she glanced at her watch, she was surprised to see that she had been on her cushion for almost an hour, longer, much longer, than she had been able to sit still in months. Her body reaped the reward of such deep relaxation, and each muscle felt as soft as butter.

"Ralph, you're looking especially pleased with yourself this morning. You're a smart dog. You know what day it is, don't you?"

"What day is it?" a little voice asked from the bottom of the steps. Ben looked up at her with a twinkle in his eye. He was learning the fine art of teasing and thoroughly enjoyed it.

"It's a good day for the zoo," Rachel teased back. "Want to go with us?"

"No!" Ben yelled at the top of his lungs. "It's our get-married day. Come on. Hurry. We've got to get ready. I need to put on my tuxebo. I shined my shoes. Wait 'til you see them. Mary helped me."

Rachel closed the door behind her and walked down the stairs toward the child waiting for her. His eyes shone with the excitement of the day ahead.

"How about we take it easy," Rachel said, ruffling his hair. "The wedding is at eleven o'clock and it's only eight. We've got three hours to get dressed. Let's have some breakfast, okay?"

"Pancakes? Can we have pancakes?"

"We don't have that much time, Ben," John said as he walked out of the bathroom. "Cheerios will have to do this morning. Why don't you let Ralph out and meet us back in the kitchen after he does his rounds."

Ben dashed off to do his favorite chore, Ralph close on his heels. John took Rachel in his arms as soon as they were alone. "I can't believe you'll be my wife in three hours. It still doesn't seem possible. You're not going to change your mind, are you? Leave me standing at the altar? Go off to Taos without me and find some good looking cowboy instead?"

"Mmmmmmm. There was that good looking young cowboy I met on the patio at Doc Martin's that time."

"Young, did you say?"

"Very young."

"I thought you liked older men."

"I do. That's why I'm marrying you instead of him."

"Did he ask you to marry him?"

"A minor detail, sir. Very minor."

Rachel offered John her lips, and they enjoyed a long, lingering good morning kiss before they went into the kitchen to pour three bowls of Cheerios and a bowl of dog food. Just as she put the milk back in the refrigerator, she heard a knock at the back door. When she opened it, Susan dashed in, carrying the paper.

"You're up! Good," Susan said, rushing past her, through the kitchen and into the living room. Still in her fuchsia pajamas and her hair in curlers, she stood in front of the fireplace, surveying the white folding chairs that had been arranged in the hall at the foot of the stairs. Several minutes later, she dashed back into the kitchen and out the back door.

"What was that all about?" John asked.

"That was all about Susan," Rachel said around a mouthful of Cheerios. "Need I say more?"

* * *

Rachel looked at her reflection in the mirror and saw a vision from another era. The cleaners had been able to restore her grandmother's wedding dress to its nearly original crisp organza whiteness. The gold locket lay flat against the Spanish lace bodice. She smiled with satisfaction at how trim her waist looked beneath the brocade bodice and the multi-layered tiers of organza billowing out around her. Now all she had to do was trade her Birkenstocks for the white satin pumps Susan had insisted she buy to complete the ensemble.

Her silver braid hung down her back, a garland of bridal veil crowning her head. She wore the Scooby Doo ring on her right hand, leaving the left finger ready for the simple circle of diamonds John would place there after they said their vows.

She listened as her friends chatted downstairs. The string quartet had begun the music that preceded the wedding march. The ceremony was to be short and simple, ending with a wedding poem Susan had written.

Rachel peered down at the scene below her. On the front row, Susan, Jim, Georgia and her husband sat with George, Belle, Mary and Nancy and Simon from the farm. Deejee and Belinda from the

All Good Things

Phillips Gallery, Mr. and Mrs. Moser from next door sat behind them. She was surprised to see Horace Junior with Carrie. A few of John's co-workers and family filled in the remaining seats.

"Guess it's time," Rachel said to Ralph. "You got the rings?" She leaned down and felt for them in the little bag tied to his collar. "Yes, looks like you're doing your job."

Rachel and Ralph slowly descended the stairs as the musicians started playing the first notes of the wedding march. Everyone rose from their chairs and turned to face the bride and her dog as they walked toward John in front of the fireplace.

She heard Susan sniffle. Mr. Moser blew his nose.

"Dearly beloved, we are gathered together . . ."

The service went off without a hitch. Ben came forward to remove Rachel's ring from Ralph's pouch and gave it to his grandfather on cue, and Mary followed his lead when it was time for Rachel to give John his.

The two children stood together and held hands for the blessing of the rings. When Rachel caught a glimpse of them out of the corner of her eye, she felt her own sniffle begin and was thankful Susan had loaned her a lacy handkerchief. When Georgia's minister said, "Ladies and gentlemen, I give you Mr. and Mrs. John Turner," Rachel couldn't believe the service was over so quickly. The sound of clapping – and John's lips on hers –assured her it was.

"I love you, Rachel Turner," he whispered in her ear.

She hugged him to her tightly. "I love you, John Turner."

The two led the small group into the dining room for a champagne toast and cutting of the cake. As everyone finished the last crumbs, Susan pushed her way through the crowd surrounding the wedding couple.

"Rachel, Rachel, we almost forgot," she hissed. "The bridal bouquet. Where is it? You forgot to toss it. Everyone back into the hall. Everyone except Rachel, back to the stairs."

Susan retrieved the delicate arrangement of white roses from the top of the refrigerator where Rachel had laid it, shoved the bride back up the stairs, and turned her around with her back to the friends gathered below her.

"What do I do now?" Rachel whispered.

"You toss it over your shoulder, silly. The lucky lady who catches it will be the next to get married." Susan ran down the steps to join the small group of women waiting for the toss.

"One, two, three," Rachel shouted, throwing the bouquet over her shoulder. It soared out from her hands in a perfect arc, landing in the middle of a tangle of hands clutching at the stems, the ribbons, the petals.

When Rachel turned around to see who had successfully held on to the flowers – successful, if the saying were true, in love – the person she saw clutching the roses to her heart was Belle.

Mary grasped one of the ribbons that trailed from her mother's hand, and Ralph and Ben ran around them in circles. George stood nearby, smiling at the Disneyesque scene in front of him. Finally, he turned to Rachel and mouthed the words "thank-you" just as the guests filled the hallway with applause.

The End

Acknowledgments

Thanks to all the many readers of *It All Started with a Dog* who loved Rachel and her story so much that they encouraged me to write this sequel. While at times, the question "Have you finished the second book yet?" felt like a thorn in my side, I am grateful now that you didn't give up asking and that the thorn is fully realized now as this complete rose of a book.

Special thanks to Mike Simpson, publisher at Indigo Sea Press, who offered to take a look at the sequel when it was written. He gave me the incentive to do what so many others had suggested.

I appreciate all the book clubs members who inspired me with ideas for the continuation of the story and who had confidence that I could tell it. In many ways, writing the sequel was harder than the first book because of its heartfelt reception by readers hungry for a feel-good story.

Surely, "All good things come to those who wait."

Leigh Somerville

About the Author

Leigh Somerville lives in Winston-Salem, NC. Photo courtesy of Daniel Alvarez.

Despite the good intentions of match-making friends, family, and neighbors, Rachel Springer, a tough Washington, D.C. lawyer, has spent a lifetime protecting her heart from the dangerous possibilities of love. When she finds a ragged stray dog on the streets of Georgetown and brings him home with her, she starts a sequence of startling events that lead her down a path she's never explored. Along the way, she rents her downstairs apartment to a bachelor whose 5-year-old grandson has the same effect on her as the homeless dog. Rachel's expanded life in Washington takes several unexpected turns as she juggles the dramas of divorces and molestation charges; a midnight drunk on her front porch; a health crisis that threatens to disrupt her lawfirm; and a weekend tragedy that turns her world upside down. All it takes to fully open the door to Rachel's heart is the disappearance of the dog that started it all.